THE RED SOFA

THE
SEAGULL
LIBRARY OF
FRENCH
LITERATURE

THE RED SOFA

Michèle Lesbre

Translated by Nicole and David Ball

LONDON NEW YORK CALCUTTA

This work is published with the support of
Institut français en Inde – Embassy of France in India

Seagull Books, 2021

Originally published in French as *Le canape rouge*
© Sabine Wespieser éditeur, 2007

First published in English translation by Seagull Books, 2016
English translation © Nicole Ball and David Ball, 2016

ISBN 978 0 8574 2 876 9

Typeset by Seagull Books, Calcutta, India
Printed and bound by WordsWorth India, New Delhi, India

I used to think that people's lives were a swift silvery trail, like the trail of shooting stars. Then one day, we don't know why, their eyes fall into darkness, never to be seen again.

Luc Dietrich

The Happiness of Sad People

Life moves, travels; and above the villages and the remote countryside, while the trains of time ceaselessly go by, one after the other, above the deserted villages and the silent countryside remains the dear, admirable, faithful utopia.

Anna Maria Ortese

October 1991

To the old gentleman
at the Gambetta station.

*

On a dirt road, a man was rolling a cigarette. He was standing by his green sidecar, a gigantic Beetle, a companion in solitude. The man and his machine, together. I could recognize his gestures from afar— Gyl used to roll his own cigarettes, too. He would keep the pinch of tobacco in the hollow of his hand, crumble it with his fingertips, spread it over the fold of the paper and close the whole thing after a little lick of the tongue on the edge of the gummed paper. The smell of honey and hay floated in the air, even though I was behind the window of the compartment and the man about ten metres away. I could almost hear the rustling of the tobacco, I could imagine the deft fingers, the absent-minded, mechanical gesture. A suspended moment in time, an intimate ritual. Not so much a glance for the train that was gathering speed again and I thought that's what travel was like, too, waking up somewhere in Siberia, but where? To see a man rolling a cigarette, to lose him from view very quickly and to remember him always. Even today, I sometimes think of the brief apparition of that stranger I caught in a private moment and of others who have mysteriously settled into my memory, like silent witnesses of my wanderings.

I was at a point in my life when the insistent presence of the world, the lack of power of all discourses and worn-out theories tormented my days and my nights. It seemed I had nothing to hold on to, time wanted to swallow me up, was swallowing me up. At any rate, it felt like all our hopes were slowly, inexorably reaching an end. I was not the only one to perceive that insidious erosion of the certainties which had filled our youth with enthusiasm, but what really frightened me was the feeling, shared by some of my friends, of being unable to do anything but sink into this realization. In a novel about the death of theories, I had read: 'We wonder just how seriously we had taken them.' I resented the author for his cruel hypothesis. That world we dreamt of, that lovely utopia—to be oneself, completely oneself, but also to transform all of society—could that be mere childishness? Was that merely consoling us for being the orphaned heirs of the crimes committed in Eastern Europe and elsewhere, crimes that some of our elders had pretended to be unaware of?

As for Gyl, he didn't want to abandon everything that had lent meaning to his life up to then, the idea of building an ideal world. On a whim, he had gone to live at the edge of Lake Baikal, to paint, perform plays with the people there and put on plays by Vampilov who had spent his whole career in Irkutsk. His choice worried me, but I could understand how both symbolic and desperate it was. No point trying to hold him back, no one and nothing had ever held him back. For the first six months he had written often, telling me he had time to go fishing for omul in the lake and make kites for the children.

And then, silence.

After weeks without hearing from him, I had decided to make the same trip on the same train. We hadn't shared our daily lives for a long time but we had shared a lot together. The idea of him being in any kind of danger threw me into unspeakable anxiety. Perhaps the man standing near his motorcycle was a sign that I was drawing near to Gyl. Those familiar gestures could be proof; I needed to convince myself of it.

I had left without telling anyone except for the magazines I was working for and the old lady in my building, seated on her sofa at the end of the long hallway. I was thinking of her as I walked through the corridor in the train to get to the samovar. Same worn rug, same faded curtains. I was sure she didn't miss me. In a way, with her failing memory, she was the absent one, alone except for a few women helpers who came every day to attend to her in that apartment, immobile behind its closed doors. Twice a week I would go down one floor to read to her a bit, or to tell her about the life of women who were dear to me because of their insolence, their courage, their

sometimes mischievous mind and, often, because of
their tragic fate. The reading would put her to sleep
but those extraordinary lives held her attention so
much that sometimes she took herself for Marion du
Faouët, Olympe de Gouges, Milena Jesenská or Anita
Conti, that woman who photographed the high seas
and pursued her passion to a ripe old age. They all
revived her—at some point she would get up, eager
for the animation of the real world out there, for
adventure. We would walk downstairs arm in arm to
go have a drink at the cafe across the street and then
hobble back up the stairs to the red sofa, where I
would leave her in a state of gentle euphoria.

In the corridor of the train, a few kids would wait
for me to get me to say two or three words in Russian.
Invariably, my bad pronunciation made them burst
out laughing. I sometimes imagined her sitting
between her cushions, the rowdy rooftops of Paris at
her back, behind the window she never opened. I wondered if in her boredom she was able to summon up
our friends without me, especially Milena, her
favourite. She would often lose herself in all those agitated lives and couldn't remember which one swam
across a river to get to a date on time—a story she
adored. Her solitude was what drew us together, and
that attachment, which originally came from living
next door, had gradually become so important that I
wondered what had driven me one day to ring her

doorbell. So in a way she was part of my voyage, a voyage that from time to time I feared was senseless, lacking any real destination, or worse, with an obscure destination, like the one in Yuri Buida's *The Zero Train*.

I had already noticed a few deserted stations in the middle of nowhere, where Buida's old Ardabyev may have been bewailing so much isolation and the hidden meaning of those departures of armoured cars with no returns. 'Secrets are always meant to harm people.'

Then I'd think of Gyl, of the kites he held up high like those banners we used to hold up long ago. I imagined them looking like large, melancholy birds over the lake. I thought of the faraway time when we made love and all of life was still ahead of us—and of all those years since, impalpable, as if dissolved into thin air. I knew that the return trip is the real journey, when it floods the days that follow, so much so that it creates the prolonged sensation of one time getting lost in another, of one space losing itself in another. Images are superimposed on one another— a secret alchemy, a depth of field in which our shadows seem more real than ourselves. That is where the truth of the voyage lies. The hardest thing, then, is having to get up with nowhere to go. I didn't know that when I returned, I would be spared that ordeal and would go meet someone several days in a row on a quay of the Seine.

*

Most of the time I would wake up very early, at the break of dawn. Pines and birches were hardly emerging from an ocean of fog in which the train ran blindly and a few swarms of grey *isbas* floated—their wood, worn by the frost and the brutal summer sun, looked like papier mâché. The dull light became progressively brighter, revealing a dizzying sky. I would follow it with my eyes until it took refuge at the horizon. What horizon? Everything seemed far away, inaccessible, too vast.

I liked waking up with no reference points, in that subtle mix of dream and reality. In the compartment, the irregular breathing of my fellow travellers, still asleep, added to the strange impression of being lost but, moreover, I was in a huge state of abandonment in which my body took all its space and became more receptive, more present, as the days went on.

The ceaseless, monotonous flight of the landscape plunged me into a torpor from which I only escaped by going to get a little tea, leaning on the windows of the corridor or engaging in chaotic conversation that often ended in irrepressible collective laughter.

Sometimes, the forests lost in that great silence reminded me of the tragic desolation of a battlefield.

The birches bowled over by the winds and the harsh winters resembled wounded giants transformed by the whiteness of their trunks into evanescent silhouettes. The villages, with their dachas surrounded by fences, were identical: a goat almost always tied to a fence, a few rare herds of cows, a few ponds and a few marshes. A cemetery was huddled at the edge of a wood, and the graves surrounded by metal railings meant, perhaps, that in such a vast space, the desire to delimit one's own—even the space of death—was irrepressible. Then the heavy figure of a woman wearing a headscarf, boots and shapeless clothing, carrying a bucket, a bag or some tool or other would suddenly appear. The babushka. Where could she be going? Probably towards that *tomorrow maybe* I'd heard so often since I arrived in this country.

I had quickly conformed to what seemed to be the norm on the train where, clearly, everyone had put on what they ordinarily wore at home. We were settling into time. No surprised glances at the pyjamas I was sporting, even when we had to get off at a station to buy a few things. A whole train would then emerge from its sleep and spread out between the shacks of *produkty* looking for things to eat, a short period of turbulence that resembled a play break, under the vigilant eyes of the conductors. There was an odd pleasure in remaining curled inside the gentle warmth of the same garment, a refuge that became a bit more dubious-looking every day, true, but which allowed us to recognize each other: the woman in the pink dressing gown, the man wearing overalls stained with paint—Andrei, who frenetically turned out watercolours in his compartment and gave all the kids a picture drawn on the fly and endlessly repeated, in which an *isba*, a birch tree and a goat stood peacefully side by side.

Those uncertain mornings in no definite place, at no precise or even approximate time, somewhere in an indeterminate length of time, propelled me well beyond the visible landscape. The dilapidated stations made me think of other countries, sometimes ones to which I had never gone, improbable places weighed down by a sense of disturbing desolation where some tragedy was happening, unknown to the world.

I insisted on asking questions about the many abandoned factories, about the housing projects built next to them, abandoned as well. All I got were evasive replies. My curiosity didn't shock them but I realized how naive it seemed, for questions that have no answers are useless; they had learnt that a long time ago, and their smiles forgave me for so much innocence.

In some towns, the platforms would be overflowing with a compact crowd with bulky baggage. The exodus of poverty? A last-ditch attempt to escape?

Sometimes it was hard to feel at ease in my status as a light traveller. I was only passing through. Aside from the basic necessities, I had two books to sustain me: one by Jankélévitch which had accompanied me for months, and the other, *Crime and Punishment*, which I had decided to read again during the trip, in a new translation. In the philosopher, I found that ineffable poetry with which he evoked the tragedy of life; and in Dostoevsky, what I thought I could read on certain faces, the exhausting history of this country, its dark mood, its excessiveness, its cruel savagery, but its greatness, too—a storm frozen in the blue-grey eyes of the Russians. 'I have a plan: to go mad', he had written to his brother one day, words that prowl through the wild despair of Raskolnikov, whose violence I soothed by rereading a few sentences of Jankélévitch. So as the hours went by, I went from the tormented sky of St Petersburg and its Haymarket Square to crystalline moments when everything was bathed in a light so intense it became unreal. Sometimes I had the confused impression that I had embarked on a strange adventure in which the lady sitting on her red sofa was doggedly pursuing me, arousing in me a vague sense of remorse.

In this slow drift into another state, I had several ways of not losing all control—taking notes, deciphering the names on the front of stations: Kirov, Ekaterinburg, Novosibirsk . . . 'Seeing landscapes through the window means knowing them doubly—through the eyes and through desire,' Milena wrote in one of her columns.

I was carried along by desire, a desire increased every day by my worry about Gyl. He had made this trip before me, his eyes had wandered through these landscapes, on these railway platforms and he must have given himself to daydreaming before those passing birches, pines, disembowelled factories, marshes and skies set ablaze in the evening just before nightfall, when the light becomes iridescent.

I was not running after an old love, but it was as if he represented all the others, as if he contained them all in one story that resembled me, plural and singular at the same time. The old lady seemed to follow me on the train—I thought of her often. Each in our own way, we were going towards the moments in our life where it had all begun.

*

I had never run into her in the lobby of the building, nor on the stairs. I knew all the other people who lived there, or at least their names and faces, but Clémence Barrot remained a mystery. No sound would ever reach me when I walked by her door, and if I asked questions about her, all I got were laconic answers and knowing looks . . . A character! She had lived in her apartment for a very long time, which made her the senior resident—justified by her age, too. I hadn't lived there for very long.

One day, pretexting a dinner at my place, I went downstairs and rang the bell at the apartment on the third floor, left, and apologized in advance for any possible disturbance, however unlikely, as we were going to be no more than three or four people at the table. A young woman appeared and a voice coming from the depths of the apartment asked, 'What is it?' Without waiting for the girl's answer, I introduced myself. 'Your neighbour from upstairs.' 'Come in!' I crossed the threshold and saw her at the end of that narrow, dark hallway, with its window opening on a bit of sky. The red sofa was placed in front of it. 'Come here!' the frail silhouette ordered.

I suggested, jokingly, that she give me a forfeit to pay if we were making too much noise that evening.

With a big smile, she retorted that she would rather we proceeded differently: for all past dinners, for this one and the next ones, she would only ask in exchange that I occasionally read to her a little, if I had the time. Taken aback at first, I remained silent, but then I volunteered for the next day at the end of the afternoon, adding that it wasn't a forfeit but a pleasure.

'What do you like?' 'Whatever *you* like,' she answered. I spent hours wondering what text I would start these sessions with. I got up several times during the night to explore my library, and at dinner I asked my friends what they thought. They were of no help and even laughed at my new vocation.

The next day I rang at the third floor left again, with Virginia Woolf, Carson McCullers and Hélène Bessette in my pocket, but this first meeting was devoted to introductions. As soon as I arrived, she left the sofa, planted herself in front of the nearest door and opened it without even saying hello to me. 'This is what my whole life was like,' she said. A milliner's workshop appeared, an organized jumble that might make you think it was still in use. A long table was cluttered with wooden moulds and, on a few of them, something that still had the shape of a hat. She didn't say hat but 'bonnet'. 'Oh, did I make bonnets!' Aside from a number of irons, many accessories of all kinds were scattered on the table: feathers, pearls, cloth flowers, ribbons, various edgings, braid shiny or dull, satin leaves as well as fabrics piled up in a corner and boxes of unused felt.

She walked to a huge closet, turned the key and revealed her treasure to me: thirty odd 'bonnets', each more extravagant than the other, little coloured jewels, plumed, feathers, in the most varied, amusing shapes. 'Would you like to try one on?' 'All of them, of course!' And she sat me down on a stool facing the mirror that hung on one of the doors of the closet. So we went through all those marvels she had made with her own hands: a perky pink panama hat with a little veil and dove-wings on the sides, a black velvet toque with an ostrich plume, a lamé turban (she claimed she made one of the famous turbans worn by Simone de Beauvoir, and occasionally worked for Balmain and Balenciaga), a perky beret to tilt over one eye, a wide-brimmed hat made of rice straw, and a moire croissant-shaped hat, moss green, decorated with a bouquet of shantung autumn leaves. At the end, we were just two girlfriends having fun together. Our laughs piqued the curiosity of the young woman who came knocking at the door once or twice. 'Everything's fine, dear,' the old lady answered.

'Which one would you like?' The offer embarrassed me, but I realized I should absolutely not refuse it. I took the pink panama.

Then we chatted for a long time in the hallway. She, sitting on her sofa, and I on the chair that would afterwards become my territory. At each of my visits, that chair seemed to be waiting for me, along with her.

She wanted to know who I was, what I did and how I lived. She liked my name, Anne, and made me promise to tell her about the women I told her I was writing of in magazines; she then asked me if I had a husband. I answered that I was not married, that I could never see myself married, but . . .

She interrupted me, slipped a hand between the seat and the back of the sofa and pulled out a photo in which a young Clémence Barrot was sitting, legs dangling, held close by a boy of the same age, on a quay of the Seine. It was nice out, it seemed, perhaps it was even summer; she was wearing a light dress and sandals and he was in a short-sleeved shirt. 'Read the back,' she said, and I read aloud: 'Paul and Clémence, 1943.' 'You see, I know all there is to know about loneliness; he died ten days after that Sunday, shot on a street corner with one of his comrades in their Resistance network. He was nineteen, only nineteen.' And she put the snapshot back in its place. We never spoke about Paul after that—his presence was so strong that there was no need to mention it. I knew he was sleeping between the seat and the back of the sofa and I imagined Clémence's hand reaching for him several times a day. But a few months later she had forgotten him and the hiding place, too. And yet, the photo I showed her woke something up in her. Her face would cloud over, her silence groped for words that didn't come, except for the day when, in a subdued voice, she said I loved him, as she had at our first meeting and then I had asked, 'Was he the only one you ever loved?' 'I loved them all,' she'd answered. 'So did I,' I murmured, and we exchanged a look I would never forget, a look that attached us to each other, already.

*

The people in the compartment were named Tania, Vassili, Piotr, Vera, Boris and Vanya. At times they would appear and disappear and that made it impossible to exchange a word with them. They were all no more than furtive shadows, especially at night, when the train stopped somewhere and they would come and go in the silence and mystery of their lives. Their bodies would stretch out, discreetly get up, then slip away and vanish into one of those cities of which nothing could be seen, only a vague outline emerging from the semi-darkness or the still-thick veil of dawn. This perpetual movement would make each encounter both fleeting and crucial. Their faces would fade with time, but the men and women with whom I came into contact made an impression that would never leave me.

They were all surprised at my presence there: Why hadn't I taken the tourist train instead of this crawler?

I explained that it was less expensive and it gave me a chance to meet them, otherwise, I might have travelled across Siberia without saying a single word of this language that I'd made the effort to learn, at least a little.

When I revealed the true goal of my voyage—to find a friend in Irkutsk or by the banks of Lake Baikal, I was met with incredulous glances and puzzled smiles. Most of them travelled thousands of kilometres to find jobs, sometimes with their family but mostly alone, leaving behind a life and loved ones. The women travelling with their children dragged mountains of bags and bundles with them. They lived on the train as if they were at home, running from the samovar to their compartment, improvising meals with whatever they bought on the station platforms, in shops or from the peasant women who came to sell their products: meat rolls, cooked potatoes, pieces of roasted chicken. Domestic smells floated through the crowded corridor. Children made plans to meet there, men escaped, their eyes following the headlong flight of the forests.

A woman and her son, a tall, slender adolescent whose slightest movement seemed to terrorize his mother, came and went in the narrow space, removed from all that surrounded them. She spoke in a low, monotonous voice and he had a lost gaze, almost blind. Both were theoretically seated in the compartment next to mine, but for three days and three nights I saw them wandering, one behind the other. When the boy managed to escape his mother's eyes, she would rush after him and they would resume their obsessive perambulations. Sometimes the conductor, a young woman, suggested they stay in the compartment to sleep a little. They were tireless and stubborn. From time to time, they would disappear for a while but very soon they were back again in that unchanging order, with him in the lead closely followed by his mother, whose face was crumpling before our very eyes. They got off at daybreak at a shunting yard in the middle of the wilderness, and vanished into the fog.

All the stations were on Moscow time, all of them, and very soon I gave up calculating what time it was. The passing hours weren't time, just a flight, a moment of respite, perhaps, for I couldn't forget that I was travelling through the tunnel of silence Gyl had dug behind him. The regular rhythm of the train was taking hold of me. Its panting, its sighs, something alive, tangible and carnal, created an intimacy that I sometimes found in the glances I exchanged with the other passengers.

Still, I sometimes had an irrepressible urge to be alone. I would roll myself up in the sheet and try to isolate myself, but there were six of us in the compartment almost all the time, and even if we all did our best to respect the five others, our rhythm was not the same. Suddenly it became impossible to stand the smells of food, the conversations that stretched on endlessly in a language I hardly knew. Then I would withdraw and bury myself again in

Raskolnikov's tormented soul. I waited for the city of Tomsk through which Michael Strogoff had gone, thought of Chekhov (I was planning to visit the house where he'd lived in Irkutsk) and of the theater in Vorkuta, that gulag in the far north of Russia where his plays and the plays of other authors were performed because Stalin wanted the life of the prisoners (the *zeks*) to be *joyful*! I thought of Medvedkin's film-trains in which workers and peasants acted as themselves and I thought of his film, *Happiness*, in which a woman sent her man out in quest of that beautiful delusion, thus throwing him into a series of misadventures as funny as they were cruel. Then, I'd think of Gyl, who had left in quest of that same mirage. If my visible luggage was minimal, I carried other baggage in my head and sometimes it would overwhelm me and take me back to my worries.

And then, one morning, Igor arrived.

*

I had just read 'There are encounters with people completely unknown to us who trigger our interest at first sight, suddenly, before a word has even been said . . .' But Igor was not one of Dostoevsky's characters, he reminded me more of the Tarkovsky character called the Stalker. In fact he was totally that character—that apparent fragility in a solid body, that juvenile pallor on a face already marked by time.

He settled into the bunk that Vassili had vacated a short time ago, right in front of mine. Without even taking off his worn leather jacket, he stretched out and slept like a log for a whole day. Intruders must have visited him in his sleep for he grunted and sighed from time to time. I watched him, imagining a cold light somewhere, in a room handed over to shades, and then the Zone and the Room, that whole solitude of the two men who accompanied the Stalker into the tunnel saying 'Everything has meaning, a meaning and a cause.'

Igor had explained to Piotr that he was going to Ulan-Ude. A job as a mechanic was waiting for him there, a job his brother had found him. So he would get off after me, and I liked that idea of a presence that would last, even if at first the man was not very talkative. When he awoke, he got up and disappeared. After a few hours, I went looking for him. I found him in the car pompously called Dining Car, seated in front of a bowl of soup that smelt strongly of cabbage, and surrounded by beer cans. He was joking with the cook, whose tight apron made his belly bulge. They were alone there. The tables covered with stained tablecloths were dancing along with the train and losing their pots of artificial flowers that rolled along the floor with a strange sound.

The two men stopped talking when they saw me but immediately resumed their conversation. I ordered a cup of tea and sat down at the next table, hoping to initiate some kind of exchange. 'Are we still far from Zima?' The cook shrugged and put on a doubtful face; Igor was staring at his plate and gulping down his soup. He was ignoring me. The other, apparently less hostile, shot me furtive glances which, when I met his eyes, seemed lacking in amiability. From time to time, he would disappear behind a partition from which a veritable concert of pots and pans would suddenly burst forth, competing with the strident complaints of the train and the noisy rolling of the flowerpots that kept criss-crossing the car. Then, rubbing his hands against his apron, he would suddenly reappear, take a couple of beers out of its pocket, set them down on Igor's table and sit down in front of him again.

I was drinking dark, bitter tea while trying to catch a glimpse of the landscape, hidden behind the drawn curtains. Always the same thing and yet I had the constant impression that it was different, almost unexpected. A limitless immensity where my own limits were erased, where I lost that slightly dizzying, disquieting feeling of distance. I was forgetting myself or, more precisely, I was caught up by the kind of dizzying solitude and inebriation travel can create, that momentary obliviousness of habits and points of reference.

Summer was waning, and at the end of the day an intense light would fall from the sky, making the trunks of the birch trees almost phosphorescent and the colours saturated. Night would fall all at once, dense, full of nostalgia and strange agitation, tinged with that inexpressible, almost animal anxiety before dark, an ocean of darkness.

But they were indifferent to the sudden arrival of night. They would exchange jokes I could not understand. Their laughs covered the clanking of the train and the flowerpots pitching around, continuing their mad race beneath the tables in the midst of total indifference. The cook would get up at regular intervals to stir the pots in the kitchen and bring out more beers. An odd atmosphere pervaded the car; you would have thought we had wandered into some dive at the very end of the earth.

A few customers had come in. They had settled around several tables, breaking up the unusual trio we were forming.

The cook had disappeared again; the pots resumed their racket and a smell of cabbage invaded the car. Igor got up and joined his pal; I could hear their voices over the general noise and the resonant wanderings of the flowerpots. Then he came back, carefully holding a steaming plate, set it in front of me with a vague smile and made a gesture meaning it was delicious before turning on his heel without even giving me the time to thank him. The cook, beaming, motioned to convey that the soup was a gift . . .

When I got back to the compartment Igor was asleep, unless he was pretending. I opened *Quelque part dans l'inachevé*, the words that Jankélévitch had taken from Rilke seemed to speak to me of this voyage and I read 'We need clandestine skies and magical causality which escape the prosaic obligations of the day.'

Igor was already awake, he had gotten up and was leaning on the windowsill in the corridor.

'Tell me about that gutsy girl again,' Clémence Barrot would sometimes ask about Marion du Faouët and her army of brigands. She had, just as I did, a real affection for that child who had not grown up to become a lady's companion despite all the efforts of the Jaffré sisters, the ageing unmarried descendants of a ship-owner of Port Louis, who had applied their principles of education on the impoverished girl. No, she became a leader of men instead, an avenger of Brittany which had been starved during the 1740s. Rather than submitting to good manners, she preferred to slip out and go drink with Irish sailors at the port. As a child, she would follow her mother to the fairs to sell ribbons and laces. Later, Marion brought her mother into her band, as well as her brother Corentin and her soon-to-be lover, Henri, her 'unfortunate lord', who took her down with him when he was captured. This fine team roamed through the countryside on horseback, robbing the bourgeois, the merchants and the priests, distributing the loot among the destitute and merrily celebrating each expedition. A wild beauty, faithful to her village, her loves and her ideals, Marion had been imprisoned several times before dying on the gallows at the age of thirty-eight.

For Clémence, thirty-eight was the age when she went into business for herself in her apartment. She first lived there for a few years with the man she called Gaby, then alone, but also with some love affairs that punctuated that long period without Paul. Now that she only occupied the narrow hall and that red sofa on which she looked like a museum guard, everything was all jumbled up in her memory, I could feel it. My visits, my readings and those women I introduced her to stimulated her. She travelled through those lives as if in a dream, confusing her life and theirs.

Each time, we would go down to the cafe and raise a glass to them—to our loves, too, for we would talk of love a great deal, with a freedom that delighted me so much that I read her the answer that a certain Mary Kesteven had given, in 1946, to the question asked by the magazine *Le Miroir Infidèle*, 'What do you love above all?' 'Making love, the earth after rain, making love, alley cats, making love, flowers, making love, a few rare children, making love, people who know how to judge themselves, making love, rivers, making love, ports, making love, cleanliness and kindness, making love.'

Clémence would laugh, a crystalline laugh, something childish and joyous . . . Love! She would repeat, closing her eyes, then whispering that with Paul she would have made a swarm of children. I also read her that same Mary Kesteven's answer to another question: 'What do you fear?' 'Many responsibilities, having to live in a country that worships machines, fatigue, crowds, idiots, boredom, too much work, seeing dogs run over, horses falling and men throwing up.'

A shadow had gone through her eyes and I took her hand, a tiny hand. That gesture calmed her down. I would have liked to take her in my arms: I've always been frightened by the distress of ageing bodies that no hand caresses, that is never embraced, the immense loneliness of the flesh which is already something like death. As a child, I was fascinated by my grandmothers' skin, I would touch it cautiously, as if I were afraid of crumpling it still more, of tearing it under my fingers, of my clumsiness precipitating a fatal outcome. Clémence Barrot's skin, thin and diaphanous, reminded me of those infinitely tender moments when I would lose myself in the geography of the wrinkles and blue veins—little wandering, palpitating streams—that ran over the damaged hands of those women. I couldn't imagine them as the little girls they said they had been. I attributed those anecdotes to their imagination, and they had a lot of it, always inventing tall tales for me. So their childhood was part of those fables you pretend to believe in, fables that remain in our memory for a long time after the voices have gone silent.

The day we were talking about Mary Kesteven, we had gone down to the cafe. It was a beautiful afternoon; Clémence was wearing a mauve dress and a pearl necklace that matched the white of her hair. I could see that smile again, the one she had in the snapshot with Paul. Perhaps she was thinking of him, for while we sipped our glasses we were silent, a peaceful, complicit silence. That woman was entering my life noiselessly; perhaps she was giving me the chance to tame that dreaded time of old age that was in wait for me.

*

Standing in the corridor, Igor was looking out at the night. The way he had peered at it during the three nights that preceded my arrival in Irkutsk. During the day he would lie down and sleep between two incursions into the dining car. I remember that when I got back, sitting on a quay of the Seine, the images of the journey mingled with the light of the pale autumn sun and I had the impression I was seeing them floating on the surface of the water. I thought I could make out Igor's silhouette carried away by the current, as the train had carried us away. Silent, enigmatic Igor.

From my bunk, I would observe his motionless back, the nape of his neck, his almost completely shaven head, his shoulders moved by a slight quivering, a hardly perceptible little jolt. I didn't know why he was the one I felt like talking to right away, telling him about my short stay in Moscow before leaving for Irkutsk. But had he even gone to Moscow? Had he crossed the Red Square, visited the Pushkin Museum and the Museum of the Revolution, walked up and down Arbat Street? How could we share something when I was simply passing through this country and he was carrying all of its history inside his body? He wasn't out on a jaunt, and the few

words I knew would have been powerless to over-
come that distance between us. I had spent two days
in Moscow as a tourist, a summary approach to a city
where I knew no one, where my references were literature, film and history. I had the impression of ver-
ifying what my imagination had constructed which,
perhaps, justified my presence in that city.

Igor's motionless silence excluded me and ren-
dered pathetic my wanderings over the square where
St Basil's Cathedral, the History Museum, Lenin's
tomb, the GUM department store and the vicinity of
the Kremlin attracted me at all times of day. So much
so that I would get up with the sun to try to be alone
on the square and return late in the evening, before
going back to my hotel near Arbat Street, a street full
of women who trained dogs or sold kittens piled up
in lace-decorated baskets, peddlers crying their
wares, musicians, fashionable girls and mafiosi
hidden behind the tinted windows of Mercedes.
Mayakovsky had committed suicide in this neighbourhood many years ago. It was already another
century.

On the square, I sometimes had in my mind
the black-and-white stories of a weekly I used to
read as a teenager where the grey coats, shapkas and
dark felt hats of the apparatchiks controlled the offi-
cial parades, whereas this colourful decor had something dreamlike about it. The wild architecture of

the cathedral, a match for the megalomania of its originator, Ivan the Terrible, contributed to that impression.

A little man who seemed to earn his living by cultivating a vague resemblance to Lenin transformed everything into mediocre folklore. I hadn't yet discovered the huge portrait of the real one on a bare hill between the Baikal and Irkutsk, painted in white, raising a friendly hand to salute his people! The travellers laughed heartily when they saw me taking a picture of it and yet nobody wanted to say why, as if they were still wary of the past. At night, in Irkutsk, the only well-lit avenues were Lenin Avenue and Marx Avenue, leaving the neighbouring little streets in darkness. Walking near the Angara before going to bed, on that wide esplanade where couples came to kiss, I'd think of Igor, of the night on the train he had not wanted to share with anybody. I would sink into the Irkutsk night with the impression that ghosts were accompanying me—the ghosts of the Decembrists, of their courageous wives who had crossed Siberia in conditions so harsh that many had perished trying to find their men, the ghosts of Chekhov and of some of his characters.

Igor never left his post and I wondered what he saw in that bottomless darkness where sometimes the pale gleam of an insomniac village was blooming, or the luminous trace of an anonymous station. But perhaps, like me, he was giving free rein to his thought, putting a little order into whatever his life was made of, somewhere in the world, as I sometimes do in moments of respite, of parentheses. And as I think back on it today, I have the feeling he was somewhat like my Stalker and he was guiding me, forcing me to probe my own silence.

The last night before I got off the train, I had followed Raskolnikov on his painful journey leading him to his last confession, and Svidrigailov to his suicide, which he tactfully called his departure for America. 'He was not thinking of anything and did not want to think. But one image rose after another, incoherent scraps of thought without beginning or end passed through his mind.' I hoped Gyl had not pictured his own journey as his last one, something his silence may well have signified. A sudden anxiety took hold of me. I got up and went to lean at the window, near Igor. Side by side, our eyes fixed on the dark immensity that was swallowing up the train, we were, it seemed to me, if not accomplices, at least in apparent harmony. But suddenly everything would become different, I was different, I was returning to my worries. The landscape, Igor's silence, the mystery of Gyl, the image of Clémence sitting on her sofa which often came to harass me— all that was opening an abyss before me. I felt like succumbing to this void.

I had stammered out my thanks for the cabbage soup. At first he hadn't answered, and then, in an almost inaudible voice, he said in his language, in Russian, 'Obligatory.' 'Obligatory' and 'Maybe' often returned in conversations here. By offering me cabbage soup, Igor meant to let me know that he was accepting my presence. I didn't dare take things any further and he probably had no wish to do so. I left him to the intimacy of his night.

*

It was my last night on the train. A long white line, a voyage in the voyage. I was wandering between the agonies of the Haymarket and the dark labyrinth that led to the Room, with the voice of the Stalker saying 'The main thing is for them to finally believe in themselves.' Igor's silhouette would melt into the dark corridor, appear and reappear in the narrow screen left by the half-opened curtains. From time to time he would light a cigarette and the wreaths of smoke would wrap themselves around him, a light bluish fog. Sometimes he would take a few steps, walking back and forth in the compartment, staring at the rug with a preoccupied look, and then return to his watch. Perhaps it was his waking presence that made me drift off elsewhere, into other places, but perhaps it was also the empty hours, the rocking of the train, the slow numbness that was coming over me little by little. And yet without him, something would have escaped me, something of myself, of my life, of what had put me onto that train in the first place, the better to catch up with me. Even today, I continue to think that he was truly a guide, a discreet angel. Did you ever come across people who seem to be put in your path on purpose, for a reason so obvious, so earth-shaking, that your whole life is all at once utterly transformed?

Thus, in the half-darkness and slight rocking of the train, images superimposed on one another, images of other journeys suddenly came to visit me, right there, in that compartment. The wretchedness and the baroque of Naples came together again before my astonished eyes, in the perpetual hum of the city in which Ernest Pignon-Ernest drew on the wall, almost under the feet of the passers-by, a Christ offered to the crowd, in pain, a crumpling body destined to be erased. From Capodimonte, the road goes down to Naples as if to finally throw itself into the arms of the sea and flee to the Island of Procida . . . Had Igor ever left his country?

Then there was Trinidad and its stony streets, the little square in front of the museum, scorching hot and deserted, the large houses pierced by sumptuous patios, the Cuban countryside, Havana and its Malecón with its long flow of marble shining like a motionless river under the age-old trees, José Marti on Revolution Plaza, monumental and immaculate, the handsome face of Che Guevara on the façade of the Ministry of the Interior, the mojitos, the monotonous speeches of Fidel, Hotel Marazul, the candy-coloured Dodges and Buicks, the Island of Crocodiles, but also the one-party system with its political prisoners, the beaches where Soviet tourists with pale bodies always grouped together, remained standing for endless minutes at a time facing the sun or turning their backs to it, to the great amusement of the Cubans. Had Igor ever walked barefoot over warm sand?

Would he have liked the little room in Venice that looked out on Rio San Marcuola bathed in a pearly light, with the water lapping beneath the window, the bed sheets like sails swelling in the wind under which two bodies were drowning? At night, in the narrow streets where the humid brick walls gave the darkness a gentle, melancholy air, would he have had that strange impression of no longer knowing in what century he was walking? Would he have cut across the lagoon to Torcello, the little end of its world? Would he have loved those immortal beauties which are the soul of the city and are slowly sinking with it, little by little, like our lives sinking into time? What meaning could the magical word 'voyage' have for him?

He was looking at the night, that dark abyss enclosing the train into which a few far-off gleams crept from time to time; suddenly it would open onto a pure sky, setting an almost lunar landscape ablaze with a strange light. Silence was perhaps what brought us closer, that man and me, the only thing we could share. I tried to convince myself of that. He had taken on so much importance during this journey that I could not accept the fact that we could be absolute strangers to one another.

At one moment, the train stopped along a birch forest; all we could see was the brilliant whiteness of the trunks. Outside, voices were calling to each other. Igor had left his post and walked towards the exit of the car. I got up to follow him, but he had already got off and the conductor standing in front of the door stopped the travellers from getting out. I could understand fragments of her explanations: several trees had fallen on the tracks. She was urging us to return to our bunks as it would probably take an hour before we could leave. Igor had not returned and I supposed he was helping to free the tracks. Then I went to sleep in that gentle state that takes over body and spirit when sleep and the wait for the other person about to return blend together.

*

And then it was daybreak, but without Igor. Was he having his first beer in the dining car with his accomplice? I was hoping he would return before Irkutsk; I couldn't imagine leaving that train without saying goodbye. Like him, I went to lean at the window in the corridor. Long streaks of fog were wrapping themselves around the tree trunks and the woods seemed to emerge from a dream. In places, a fragile light tinged the horizon, luminous suspension points that ran along with the train and traced the limits beyond which nothing more existed.

I remembered the early hours of the morning with Clémence Barrot on the Louis-Philippe Bridge. She had sent her night nurse to ask me to come as quickly as possible. It was still dark out. I had gone downstairs, worried, thinking I would find her in bed and failing, but she was already sitting at the end of her hallway, radiant, wrapped in a bathrobe as red as her sofa. Two cups of coffee were steaming on the little table next to her.

'What day is it?' she asked. As I hesitated, slightly taken aback at the question and the time she had made me get up to ask it, she went on, 'It's 7 March, and it's an anniversary for me because on 7 March 1953, thanks to what had happened the previous night, I saw Paris at dawn for the first time. Do you know what happened during the night of 6 March?' I had no idea and I was sleepy, but she didn't give me the time to go back to sleep.

'Stalin had died!'

I sat down, drank my coffee in one gulp, afraid of having to start a difficult conversation and explain that I didn't care about Stalin's death, and if he had been polite enough to die before that, it would have been better for thousands of people. In fact, I was totally wrong; Clémence couldn't have cared less about Stalin either. She began telling me about the black hats. 'At that time I was working on Rue de Châteaudun, I wasn't in business for myself yet. As soon as Stalin's death was officially announced, the orders came streaming in—all the ladies wanted black hats! Black hats! Really! They weren't about to say a mass for the comrade, were they? But the head-quarters of the Communist Party was right nearby, all draped in black! At the shop, we worked the whole night through, drinking coffee. The boss wasn't really on that side politically, but you can't argue with profits so she was licking her chops. Around five in the morning, we all went out for a moment to stretch our legs and our minds. We walked for a good hour through the deserted streets of the neighbour-hood and saw the first courageous people putting their nose outside the door. Hours of finishing touches were still waiting for us at the workshop. We were walking quickly, we looked like girls on the run. Then we got to the Seine as the sun was rising and the immense joy I felt gave Paul back to me. It was as if he was there with me, as filled with wonder as I was, I could even hear his voice; it brought tears to my eyes. That was exactly fifty years ago. I couldn't care less about Stalin's death, all those dreams had already fled. They didn't survive Paul's death.'

'Would you like us to go see the sunrise over the Seine?' I asked.

She gave me a childish smile and I went upstairs to my place to put on some clothes and call a taxi. The driver must have thought we were two madwomen, with her in a bathrobe and me with a coat thrown over my pyjamas. On the Louis-Philippe Bridge, the first chirpings of the birds, the first stirrings of the city accompanied the dawning light. Clémence showed me the spot on Quai de Bourbon where the photo with Paul was taken, back in 1943.

On that quay, I knew that a commemorative plaque quoted a sentence written by Camille Claudel in a letter to Rodin: 'There is always something missing that torments me.' Perhaps Clémence knew that sentence, too. I didn't say anything. The taxi driver was getting impatient, and we went home.

Once we were back at her place, I asked if Paul was in the Communist Party.

'He was.'

'And what about you, were you in it too?'

'Well, I was with Paul!'

A playful laugh. She remembered the scandal caused by the portrait of Uncle Joe that Picasso had made, a portrait that, in fact, had nothing particularly extravagant about it but, at the time, they didn't kid around with idols in the Party. They wanted a more realistic portrait, more faithful to the great man! And she went on: 'When the wife of a leader I knew by sight came into the shop to place an order, a wide-brimmed hat on which I had worked for hours, I said aloud, "He's dead, good riddance!" The others giggled except for Suzon, a Party activist all her life—she got up, went out and slammed the door behind her. As for me, I resented Stalin for having taken Paul from me—without the Party and all those lies, maybe he wouldn't have risked his life. I didn't know all the evil the tyrant had done over there yet. I was just thinking of the street where Paul fell one morning with his friend, ten years earlier. A street we often took together when he walked me home. Afterwards, I stopped going through it and took big detours to avoid it. I never pronounced the name of this street again and it would still be unbearable today.'

I didn't know what street she had erased from her intimate map, but I understood her; I could easily give up a country if a man with whom I had visited it had died.

Then I brought up one of my trips, to Prague. On Petrin Hill, at the exact spot where the menacing, monumental statue of Stalin used to stand, the gigantic lips and out-thrust tongue in a poster advertising the presence of the Rolling Stones in the city could be seen from afar. I told her how much I had enjoyed discovering that insolent tongue taunting a bygone past and how much that group had accompanied our activist frenzy.

Igor was certainly born after the death of Stalin, and I wondered what he would answer if I mentioned the name. Still, I would have liked to tell him how much his country had obsessed us, the cruel disillusions it had inflicted on us, and how this journey brought me back to the luminous years when the meaning of life was contained in one word—revolution. And while telling him this, I would have remembered a stay in St Petersburg two or three years earlier, and the magnificent villa built for the dancer who was the mistress of Nicolas II. From its balcony, Lenin supposedly exhorted the crowd to overthrow the world. The villa was requisitioned by the Bolsheviks in 1917, just like the old Smolny convent near which I was staying. Every evening I would walk through the peaceful gardens where I would pass the students who lived there now. I would wait for the late, brief darkening of the white nights of June to see the bridges of the Neva finally open like huge jaws to let the magical procession of boats go through. Without Igor, those confidences were impossible. He was the man of my silence, my guide, the one who was accompanying me without knowing it, and he would remain the incarnation of everything that was moving me so deeply during this voyage.

During those rather slow, rather lascivious hours, carried along through this landscape that stretched out endlessly before my eyes, I was discovering in myself an aptitude for contemplative life that I didn't suspect I had. It seemed like a good antidote to the modern world's agitation and unimaginative rigidity. I would doubtless return more serene, with a touch of scepticism and even fewer certainties.

Igor was still nowhere to be found, the dining car was empty and still resounded with the insistent noise of the liberated flowerpots. When day finally broke, the train stopped just before a station. Several women in men's pants, boots and headscarves were working on the tracks. You couldn't see their faces; they were bent over their labour, pulling wagons of scrap-iron or lifting stones or buckets filled with soil. Their gestures were heavy and reminded me of those Cuban prisoners I'd seen in a park, picking up papers strewn over the lawn using a wooden pole with a nail at the end. They had that almost disturbing slowness that spoke to me of another world in which I did not live and could never reach, despite all those kilometres I had spent trying to do so. One of the women had stood up straight and adjusted her headscarf. She was young, rather beautiful and I invented a life for her, loves, children, perhaps, even if I could read a quiet despair in her eyes.

Then the train started moving again. I was only a few hours away from Irkutsk. The factories still filed by one after the other, abandoned, and sometimes the equipment was, too—a monstrous waste and, after the sight of those women bent over the tracks, it was really maddening. The forests became the image of a possible paradise which men did not deserve and that only the trees knew how to incarnate. This grandiose, devastated landscape, heavy with melancholy, spoke to me of everything I already knew but with a force, a cruelty I had not expected. It would remain with me for several months after my return and settle into my life as other journeys had done, thus constructing a singular, imperfect, emotional and sometimes imaginary world—mine.

Before leaving the train, I went back to the dining car one last time. The cook knew neither his colleague of the night before, nor Igor. I then imagined two shadows, hounded perhaps, slipping into the woods. Were there really trees lying on the tracks when the train had stopped? What had those two

fellows been talking about as they drank their beers
in the dining car, and in what forbidden zone had
they gone to seek another life?

*

She had never travelled, never left Paris. Between her and the city, there was a visceral attachment. For years, after the workshop and the hats, whatever the season, Clémence Barrot had walked for hours on end every single day. Sometimes an appointment would decide her itinerary but most often she yielded to chance. She showed me several notebooks in which she used to write down the routes she took each day and her comments when she saw changes along the way. She would make sketches snatched from shop windows and they would later inspire her work. In some neighbourhoods, they called her the walking lady. She also had her favourite cafes, where they would serve her a glass of white wine at cocktail time without even asking her. (My guilty pleasure, she'd say.) The city was going through major changes but that didn't seem to affect her—as she no longer took walks, she didn't see them and paid no attention to what people were saying about them. The real Paris was her Paris, the one she had known in her youth, and nothing could destroy it.

A few days before my departure, I had come to see her and I had read, 'The long, fluid, invisible road. Marvelling together at banks of mist. Shuddering together in the fogs punctured by hoarse calls.

Together. With all the others. Held together by so much community. In the visible world. Separated by so much diversity in the visible world . . .' I was slowly reading Hélène Bessette's incandescent text, which prepared me for the idea of the journey. I was thinking of Gyl, of that Tibetan maxim which says that the journey is a return to the essential. And then I had fallen silent, absorbed by the anxiety that was driving me so far away, alone.

'What are you thinking of?' Clémence Barrot had asked.

'Of someone,' I had answered.

'You're lucky to have someone to think about,' she whispered.

'What about Paul? Don't you think about him any more?'

'What Paul?' she said.

I remembered that exact moment when I was walking through the streets of Irkutsk and I was filled with the same sadness, the same feeling of abandonment as when she had said those words. The idea of her forgetting Paul made me feel despair for her. I wanted to believe that she was still putting her hand between the seat and the back of the sofa to take him out of his hiding place. I was weeping at the thought, my tears blurring the city with its fragile, beautiful wooden houses sinking little by little, leaning so much they made you dizzy sometimes.

The frost, the summer heat and the absence of foundations, I was told later, were slowly swallowing them. They looked as if they were drifting on a sea of earth. I was slipping on this moving floor and was, perhaps, not far from Gyl, perhaps I was about to run into him. An unexpected fear had taken hold of me. It seemed to me that I lacked the words to justify my coming. I had run to him, that was all. How can one say those things simply, that feeling of urgency which had overwhelmed me? Of course his silence was at the origin of my decision, but it suddenly appeared to be only a pretext. He was under no obligation to write regularly—hadn't our lives gone their separate ways a long time ago?

I was lost, I was walking around in circles and I might have rushed to the station to take a train back if I hadn't heard the hoarse voice of the old woman singing 'Suliko'. Gyl had spoken to me of her in one of his letters. He said she lived right next to the house of the people who had taken him in on the first days of his arrival. In the evening, when she started singing her litany and went on for hours, shouts arose in the street asking her, in vain, to be quiet. She had lost two sons in Afghanistan. That tragedy was her madness and 'Suliko' her only refuge. From time to time, the voice would slip and the melody trail off, then begin again, even louder. I hummed along with her and remembered Anna Prucnal on stage at the

Théâtre du Châtelet with her beautiful face, her jeans and her leather jacket. A number of us had come to applaud her, as her repertoire was ours, too. Frail but tense, her body braced at the chords of the piano, her voice went straight to our hearts, she sang our hopes and our anger, the texts we loved, and we rose to acclaim her. The old woman's voice gave me the shivers and I couldn't help thinking of Anna's. That was in a faraway time.

I recognized the house very quickly. Gyl had sent me a photo in which he was sitting on the windowsill with a conquering smile on his face. Volya opened the door and invited me to enter without giving me the time to introduce myself. The decor of the room was dark, nestling behind the curtains that tried to soften the heat. Two children were playing in a corner, the television was on, a French film whose sound was covered by a voice-over, a man's, translating the lines of every character regardless of their sex. The effect was rather comical. As soon as I could say Gyl's name, the children ran up to me to kiss me and Volya raised her hands to heaven; the children missed him. I learnt that he was living in a tiny village on the shores of Lake Baikal, whose name meant 'the gardens'. You had to take a bus to cover the sixty kilometres between Irkutsk and the village, or the train. The next morning, I took the train.

*

'The lake is a great calm eye . . .' As soon as I arrived in the village, I looked for it. It was there at the foot of the last houses, solemn and clear, extraordinarily limpid. The cellulose factory that had threatened it had stopped working. Little wooden boats scratched the surface of the water, others were aligned along the banks; birds would come and land on them. Pine forests encircled it, a few little waves were hardly rippling but I knew there were sometimes storms and waves several metres high, which the first frosts kept frozen for months. A mysterious lake, venerated like a god.

Two kids were playing with kites, calling to each other; they had stopped abruptly when they saw me. I wasn't from the village, nor did I look like someone from around there. My backpack and my sunglasses clearly showed I was a foreigner. One of them had watched me for a long time before coming up to me and ask, 'You like Baikal?' I couldn't find the word to express my genuine emotion, I said *bolshoi*, big. He laughed and his friend came up to me, too. I asked if they knew Gyl and they answered at the same time, talking non-stop, showing me the kites which I suspected were of Gyl's own making, gesturing to explain that he wasn't there but lived just next door.

Both accompanied me to the house, a small, run-down *isba*, faded but still with pale-green traces on it. I asked where Gyl was and they answered that he had gone out on a boat to the island of the lake with his wife. 'His wife?' I asked, startled. 'Irina,' they answered in chorus. The house wasn't closed and they wanted to show me around. A tiny space with a bed, a stove, a few shelves crowded with dishes, books, various tools, newspapers and a few provisions. The two kids had gone back to their games and I remained there for a long time without moving, rather disconcerted. Then I settled in and went to get water to make tea before digging out some old biscuits stored away amid the stocked-up food.

The books were mostly theatre and French poetry. Claude Roy's collection *A la lisière du temps*. I looked for two lines I knew. 'I was absent from myself, rather an undecided cloud, a passer-by not too sure I really was somebody.' I remembered the exact time and place where I had read those lines, and I thought it was still an effect of the journey, of my idea of the voyage, reminiscences and echoes that surprise you and give meaning to simple anecdotes, fragments of texts you thought were buried in the clutter of memory and which suddenly surge up again, intact. Those verses had moved me deeply one day and they were catching up with me in that tiny house where Gyl's life was escaping from me, where

I was not sure I belonged. They were of great comfort to me. It wasn't the first time that something like this had happened—words, phrases read here and there had already flown to the rescue or had simply kept me company. They had always brought me real happiness. I sat down, I read Claude Roy's *Chien et Loup* aloud, to the end, with Clémence Barrot somehow there, on her red sofa, and I was certain she had not forgotten Paul.

Then I continued my exploration of the house. Several kites were piled against a wall and, right next to them, a handwritten poster announced a performance of Vampilov's *The Elder Son* that had taken place the preceding month. A few lines recalled that the author had gone out fishing one day on Lake Baikal but had never returned. He was thirty-five.

I drank my tea and went for a stroll around the village. Raspberries and all kinds of vegetables and flowers abounded in the little gardens. I introduced myself to several people, and each of them smiled broadly when I said Gyl's name. They repeated that he would be travelling for two weeks, but I could sleep at his house; he had left it open for anyone who might need it. They also gave me a few vegetables and smoked omul.

Later, at nightfall, I went back to the lakeside. A purple sky was reflected in the water. A group of children ran over, followed by a woman carrying a bucket filled with her wash. She proceeded to rinse it, while the children brushed their teeth and gums with their fingers under her watchful eye, shouting and splashing each other all the while. The woman was clearly their mother, still young despite that bunch of kids. Among them, I recognized the two children who had greeted me at my arrival; they hadn't noticed me yet. When I walked over to the group, the two boys rushed up to me to introduce me to the others. The mother, suddenly discovering my presence, left her laundry, wiped her hands on her apron and came over to say hello, then, with an authoritarian gesture, dismissed the children, who disappeared behind the houses. I was disappointed, but the little multicoloured army came back almost immediately, each child hugging a kite to his chest like a shield. They scattered over the banks of the lake and launched a swarm of giant butterflies into the sky, which had turned almost red by now. They began to glide around above us. The mother sat down next to me. We didn't speak; our heads raised to the sky, we followed the wavering kites, which some-times took an unfortunate dive into the lake. A bit later, she explained that Gyl had made one for every child in the village, everyone liked him and no one would let him leave again, and also that his wife Irina, a schoolteacher in Irkutsk, would have a child in a few months.

Over thirty years ago, early one morning on a grey November day, Gyl had accompanied me to the hospital. We had decided not to keep the child—it was too soon and there were still so many battles to be fought . . . Years later, it was too late, we were not together any more and I never felt the desire to have a child with the others. It was odd, but that memory was not painful; the kids offering me that spectacle with joyful shouts, were, thanks to him, almost our children, at least those of our utopia. But what would become of them? Then I thought of Igor.

The mother invited me over for a cup of tea. The kids followed us. I told her about the train, the days and the nights, the forests, and then I said I came from France. I could read in their eyes that the word France meant nothing to them. For them, I probably came from nowhere, and perhaps it was the same for Igor, who had asked me nothing. But that was really of no importance—what mattered was the encounter, the fugitive moment, that kind of unexpected luck travelling bestows on you. Words don't have the same value and even their absence sets off a beneficial drifting of the spirit.

Later, I went back to Gyl's house to get a blanket. I preferred to sleep at the banks of the lake. Impossible for me to slip into their bed. It was a sleepless night, one of those nights that takes you into your innermost self, into what animates and obsesses you.

It had taken this whole journey to understand that I was trying to find that buried energy again, that time of my life, gone once and for all, a time nothing could bring back, not even Gyl. But he had decided to have a child. I did not feel sad about it, I could only take the measure of the distance between us and the time that had gone by, a time I had tried to escape from for far too long.

When the day rose, I once again thought of Clémence, of the Louis-Philippe Bridge, of everything that attached me to her, whose life, it seemed to me, was hanging by a thread. In the house, I looked for photos where I might catch a glimpse of Irina, but there weren't any. I also tried to scribble a note to say I had been there without revealing the real reasons that made me come, but I didn't manage to do it. It would be easier in Paris. It was still very early when I left for the station.

*

From behind the window of the train taking me back to Irkutsk, I took pictures of the huge portrait of Lenin that spread out over the whole hillside. The apparition of Lenin waving his hand had staggered me and I grabbed my camera as fast as I could. The travellers around me giggled as they saw me take shot after shot, but I pretended not to notice. I remembered another portrait of him at the end of his life, when he was confined to a wheelchair after several strokes. There was a frightened look in his eyes as if he had had a nightmarish vision, as if, before his death, Russia's suffering was coming to torment him in his retreat where his favourite sister was watching over him, along with an army of doctors. It was a tragic portrait, suggesting something far more than mere illness. The sense of desolation that emanated from it was akin to the desolation of the devastated spaces I had travelled through a few days earlier, an immense anguish his body was expressing without words. The man whose famous question, *What Is To Be Done?*, had resonated over the whole world was no longer able to answer. According to Chagall, he had turned Russia upside down, as Chagall himself had done to some of his figures. Stalin's paranoid madness would do much worse.

I didn't really know how to interpret the laughter of my neighbours in the compartment, but I ended up joining in. I asked why they hadn't let the forest take back its own on that hill; no one answered. I imagined pines growing over the huge portrait, swallowing it little by little in the jungle of their roots, erasing that wave of his hand—moving and pathetic at the same time—the gesture of a ghost. But that was my own vision and theirs interested me more. They had stopped laughing, each retreating into a silence that I respected and associated with Igor's. I put away my camera and no further exchange took place until Irkutsk. There was something unreal about that trip at times; I was going to wake up in my apartment, go down a floor to read to Clémence or tell her the life of Alexandra Kollontai. She would like it, I was absolutely sure of that, and we would go downstairs to our cafe, the Bon Coin, to have a drink in Alexandra's honour.

As I came out of the station, I hesitated for a moment. I had to wait three days before taking a plane but I didn't want to be a burden to Volya, all the more so as she thought I was still in the village. I didn't want to bring up Gyl's life, either, as Volya may have known Irina—all this was a bit too complicated. I went to look for a hotel and in the course of my peregrinations, I came upon a market: Chinese pedlars selling all kinds of counterfeit products, and twenty-odd shoemakers sitting cross-legged on the ground, working in front of the onlookers and customers waiting barefoot or in their socks. I took a few pictures of the crowd that jostled between the stands, a noisy, bustling crowd. Back in Paris, after the film was developed, perhaps I would recognize Igor in the middle of a group, seen from behind: I knew that back well, the nape of that neck. And yet, I had walked around the market several times, I'd gone through all the lanes and hadn't bumped into him! I quite liked the possibility of discovering him in some photo later—that strange way of prolonging the encounter and the voyage.

The modest hotel was near the Angara River. These three days would make it easier for me to reconnect with my ordinary life. A magazine was expecting a piece on Alexandra Kollontai for the following week and wanted me to tell them what the next ones would be. I had actually suggested Alexandra Kollontai, but hadn't yet decided what would follow.

I tried several times to reach Clémence on the phone to tell her of my imminent return. No one picked up. I knew her aversion for what she called 'that thing', so there was no reason to worry, it would be nice to ring her doorbell and be the surprise of the day, like that late Sunday afternoon when I had unexpectedly introduced myself to her.

'Who are you bringing along today, at this time, with no warning?' she had asked, with that mocking smile of hers.

'Olympe,' I answered, 'Olympe de Gouges'.

'Another bold woman who came to a bad end!' she added, with her mischievous air.

Exactly, since she had died on the scaffold in November 1793, during the Reign of Terror. To me, she incarnated the superb stubbornness of an exalted soul. In the seventies, she was always inside our heads, a constant presence on our marches and in our chants. The illegitimate daughter of a marquis, Olympe was self-taught and, above all, a courageous woman, a rebel who feared no one and nothing. She hated Marat, challenged Robespierre, wrote plays and was opposed to violence: 'The blood of the guilty, when shed profusely and cruelly, is an eternal stain on revolutions.' She challenged the institution of marriage and wrote the first feminist manifesto, *The Declaration of the Rights of Woman and the Female Citizen*, fought against the death penalty, denounced slavery and, of course, the reaction was hatred and a desire for vengeance. Betrayed by the man who made her posters, she was arrested in July 1793 on the Saint-Michel Bridge and guillotined in November of the same year . . .

Clémence was really taken with Olympe. 'You see, Anne,' she said to me, 'all those women you bring into my place turn me into a bad girl—what a fine gang we'd make together, wouldn't we?'

Our cafe was closed on Sundays, so I had invited Clémence to come up to my place, raise a glass to Olympe and have dinner. It was the first time. She was delighted and wanted to dress up for the occasion. She arrived in a grey taffeta dress, with a pearl necklace and a cloud of powder that reminded me of one of my grandmothers who used it lavishly and collected compacts and powder puffs. A little handbag hung from her arm; she opened it and took out the photo of that Sunday on the Quai de Bourbon, saying, 'I took the liberty of bringing Paul along; he would have liked to know you'.

I remembered that evening as a shining pathway in the night. After the frugal dinner I had improvised, she visited my library, from which I drew everything I brought to her apartment. With her glasses at the tip of her nose, she had read a few titles aloud, thumbed through some books and finally asked me if I had a portrait of Milena. I actually had several of them, one from 1911 when Milena was thirteen, walking by herself on the banks of the Moldau in a pleated skirt, hat and gloves. Another showed her as a tennis player with a racket in her hand, but the one that struck Clémence showed her in all her radiant beauty, with a clear, very gentle gaze on her beaming face. That's how she had imagined her, luminous, with an irresistible charm.

Late into the night, she told me about Gaby, an accordionist at the dance halls on the banks of the Marne, a tender, amusing man who had never said 'I love you' because it was unnecessary. Their love had ended quietly, without tears and without bitterness. She had replaced him with Émile, a cabinetmaker near the Bastille who had hidden the fact that he was married; then, by Jean-Jean whom she had met through friends—this one played chess in the Luxembourg Gardens, smoked Havana cigars and fiddled around with electricity.

'What about you?' she had asked me.

'Some other time,' I'd answered, 'or else we'll get everything mixed up!' She laughed. I really liked her, that little woman who resisted old age so well and everything that comes with it and can turn it into permanent disaster. Thinking of her in my transients' hotel was such a pleasure; I was eager to see her again, soon, and tell her about my strange voyage, doubtless the strangest of all my voyages because, more than all the others, it had constantly brought me back to my life, to the simple truth of my life.

*

I remember that hotel room in Irkutsk, bright and comfortable. I also remember that at the moment I opened the door, a line of Antonioni's was in my mind: 'What I look for in people are signs of feelings.' I had said it one day to the man who, through a succession of small betrayals, was about to leave me but was afraid to admit it. We were on our last trip. As I entered the room after hours of wandering through a city where we kept getting lost, I had said those words to him as if they were mine, and he had cried. I was seeing him cry for the first time. Fatigue was making our bodies heavy; we made love in a kind of slow motion, numbly, and he kept sobbing into my neck. I would have liked those minutes to last for ever. That whole sweet melodrama separating us with infinite gentleness contained in itself alone all the time we had spent together.

I then reflected on the strangeness and sheer poverty of love. A few moments of our beautiful days together were streaming through my memory. He was walking into my neighbourhood bookstore again, I stopped paying attention to the books to follow the meanderings of that stranger between the tables, his slightest gestures, his way of opening the books, of reading a few lines with his lips silently moving. He paid no attention to my presence (we were the only customers in the store) until the moment he approached me to ask what I was looking for. I wasn't looking for anything in particular, just waiting for a surprise, for the wonderful find that might pop out of the books, but he wasn't listening to my answer, already suggesting that we take a walk along the canal.

I followed him and asked what book he had come to buy. None, he said. Every day, he gleaned a sentence or a paragraph that he would learn and put into a notebook. Little by little, this would become a book, an amazing jumble with no story, but it would encompass all stories and with each reading, something different would emerge. According to him, the beginning of truth—that is, an absolute mystery, would then appear. I asked him if he gave titles to those unusual collages and he laughed—he'd been making fun of me, it was something he had just made up to win me over. In fact, he had entered the bookstore to avoid someone he had no desire to see.

As I looked at the Angara from my window, I thought of the last trip I had taken with this man. The wide, slow river was making me feel rather drowsy. I lay down on the bed and dozed until night, an agitated rest of which nothing remained upon awaking. Later, I went down to the street, slightly dazed, but soon turned around to go back to bed.

I remained cloistered in this tiny space for the first two days, doing no more than going out for a drink or buying a few provisions. I began working on the portrait of Kollontai, wrote a few pages about my stay at Lake Baikal, about Gyl's house (and Irina's) and tried to remember the names of all the children. I was sorry not to have photographed them. I wrote that I regretted not having discovered the lake in winter, when it freezes over and trucks go across it. In past times, they would put tracks on the ice and the train could travel across the lake, too. At the end of these few notes, I wrote that I suddenly felt old but I crossed those words out immediately—they frightened me. I tried to understand in what way this trip was different and I had to acknowledge the fact that it was no longer sustained by what had initiated it but by something else, something that was forcing me to admit that it had everything to do with me, and me alone.

Travelling had always meant an attempt to find a link, however tenuous, with the world, to reject what slipped in-between the world and me: distances, languages, racism, religions—all obstacles that did not always disappear but gave it meaning. What made this one unique was the impression I had of being unable to get close to anything, of only skimming the surface, of being the prisoner of my fears, a stranger in the eyes of others. I tried to analyse this feeling, filling whole sheets of paper which I would then throw away. To calm myself down, I would read Jankélévitch but I felt, growing inside me, the same old disenchantment. I had wanted to fight it and escape that feeling by finding Gyl again and retrieve the wonderful energy that used to motivate us back then. No train could catch up with that time; so, on the third day, I went out.

It was a luminous day, with the same steel-blue sky and brutal sun. I first walked along the Angara before venturing out into the city and the outlying areas. I passed by women who sold knick-knacks, socks, gloves, small second-hand kitchen utensils, various tools and faded clothes. They were lined up on the sidewalk, standing, calling out to passers-by without great conviction. Nobody paid them any attention, and the same indifference could be read on their faces.

I didn't dare call Clémence back, she wouldn't pick up the phone, but as soon as I arrived the next day I would go see her, tell her about the train, Igor, the kids at the lake, and Gyl, perhaps. She would say, 'What about the others?' Like that day at the cafe across the street when we chatted, evoking the radiant times with men lost through the fortunes of life, the wonder of encounters and the more painful beauty of final goodbyes. She was telling me again about her last days with Gaby—the wildest, for they knew they were the last. I was moved by that woman who seemed to have lived a full life despite Paul's absence, because she was life itself and everything in her was saying that, still. The red sofa and the closed doors of her apartment were deceptive, the whim of an old lady, a pose to forget her physical problems and limitations. I missed her. Despite our different worlds and difference in age I found in her company a special kinship. I belonged to no one, to nothing, and nobody belonged to me. When I was young, I had fiercely claimed that independence. In a certain sense, through the years, and not without difficulty, I had conquered it. It had taught me the freedom without which love, more often than not, is smothered, turns into exasperation and fades away. Despite losing Paul, Clémence had known that freedom, thanks to her immense gift for happiness.

I was walking into the city without thinking about where I was going and, suddenly, the woman's voice rang out again: 'I saw a rose in the woods, could you have bloomed so far away, my Suliko?' And curiously, I saw myself back in Italy, leaving behind me the room and the weeping man who had finally fallen asleep. I didn't write a farewell note, I simply took my bags and went looking for another hotel. All that had brought us together was now separating us. It had been the same with Gyl, with others as well. Oddly enough, charm turned into resentment.

The woman was repeating 'Could you have bloomed so far away, my Suliko?' You could see a blank wall through the window; a man had thrown a bottle of beer inside the apartment, belching out insults and the woman had fallen silent. The noise of shattered glass and something falling made the man laugh, but the voice had resumed its litany. I would soon leave these streets, this country to which I would never return. I was finally finding myself in that pleasant sense of abandonment, that way of breathing and thinking differently in a foreign city, in a state of weightlessness, with the feeling of belonging to the world, to that ideal humanity I was seeking in the faces, the music of the language, the gestures, and the smallest details that link us all together in spite of everything. I was letting myself be swallowed up by the sounds, the rhythm, and the invisible current that ran through the city. The screen that had separated me and deprived me of it since I had arrived had been lifted. So now I wanted to make it all mine. I walked for hours through the smallest alley till exhaustion drove me to take refuge at the Globus, a basement cafe where they drank wine and singers and musicians performed one after the other.

*

He was not that young any more. He was furiously squeezing his accordion while singing a melody that, from what I understood, lamented a lost love. I was drinking Georgian wine and it was going to my head. The audience packed into the room accompanied the man by clapping their hands and sometimes singing along, louder than the singer, a deafening din, a tidal wave that was lifting up the walls and that disintegrated in the deafening applause. A few voices were chanting 'Boris! Boris!' He brandished his accordion, bowed with a lovely smile and began singing another tune, carrying an audience gone wild along with him. When he called for silence and asked if anyone had a special request, an uproar crashed over the room again. In a haze of smoke, I saw him walking towards me. I was sitting alone at a table, slightly apart, so I hoped I wasn't the one he was walking to, but there he was in front of me, asking me what I would like to hear. I knew—it was the song a man sang a cappella in Mikhalkov's film *Urga*. The film was a few years old already, but I had never heard that song again. I hummed the first notes of *On the Hills of Manchuria* and unleashed a new salvo of applause.

He remained planted in front of me and I discovered his face, ravaged by deep wrinkles—a moving

detail on a body that was still young, though a bit
heavy. I had so loved the naked voice of the man in
the film that I would have preferred him to just sing.
His voice was often lost in the sighing of his instru-
ment. At the end, he held out his hand, took me with
him to make a bow and I invited him to sit down at
my table. We talked for a long time; he told me about
his life in the army, his fateful stay in the region of
Vladivostok, transformed into a cemetery for nuclear
submarines. Nature had gone wild there. It prolifer-
ated abnormally, gigantically and was responsible for
the infirmities of his daughter, who was born over
there ten years or so ago. As he had volunteered for
this well-paid mission, taken his wife with him and
given her a child who would never be like everybody
else, she blamed him for this misfortune and left
him. He'd been singing here and there ever since,
barely making a living. 'What about you?' he asked.
I was at the end of a journey I had been dreaming
about for a long time, on a train that would keep
taking me further and further, all the way to a lake
that seemed inaccessible, just a legend, a myth. At
least that's what I told him. He was going to sing
again on a boat that was waiting for him, and as this
was to be my last day in Irkutsk, he asked me to come
with him and take a nocturnal excursion on the
Angara. I felt good with this man, and I accepted. We
walked to the river like two old friends not afraid
of silence. This encounter gave a breath of air to

the trip, a respiration, something simple, familiar. Thanks to Boris' presence, the city had become different, tamed, friendly—I was no longer a foreigner here, it accepted me. From time to time, he would stop and give me a few details about some neighbourhood or a particular house. He was the one who explained to me why most houses were sinking into the ground—their piles were not enough to protect them against the variations in temperature.

I asked him if he knew Moscow. He did, he had lived there in his youth, thanks to the Party. I told him of my fascination for Red Square, my vain attempts to be alone there and how much that place still spoke to me of a story that had been part of my life for many years. That made him smile. Did he know that in the summer of '68, eight people had had the mad courage to come and protest there against the intervention in Czechoslovakia? He did not. He had never gone into the Museum of the Revolution; I said I had visited it and noticed that it had many empty rooms and many people were missing—Trotsky, for example, whereas Stalin was everywhere. I pretended to be surprised by that. He didn't react, but then, after a short silence, he merely answered that for a long time he'd been living far removed from all those false hopes, the past no longer interested him and he expected nothing from the future. In the things he told me, I recognized what I thought I'd seen in some people's eyes. Now I understood them.

I asked who the woman singing 'Suliko' was. He didn't know, but he had occasionally heard her. Many things were said about her: some claimed she'd been dead for several years, ever since her sons had been killed in Afghanistan, and the house was haunted and it was her ghost that was singing instead of her! Just stories, of course . . .

On the boat, he had the same success as he did at the Globus; he interpreted traditional songs as well as some songs by the poet and singer Vysotsky. I stayed in the background, following the dark flow of the river, which mingled with the night and the sweet effervescence of my drunkenness. The end of the voyage made everything essential.

He walked me back to the hotel. Before the door, he opened his arms wide, I snuggled up against him, and we stayed in each other's arms while he sang *On the Hills of Manchuria* in a muffled voice, just a murmur that gave me the shivers and rocked me like the train. I thought of Igor, of the huge evening skies, of Gyl's child, of our wild hopes, of Clémence, and of the joy of being alive. I ran into the hotel lobby and turned around. He was no longer there, but I was sure I had not invented him.

*

'But that isn't true, is it?' Clémence had asked when
I was telling her how Milena Jesenská swam across
the Moldau because she wanted to be on time for
her date with Ernst Pollak. I added that later, when
Pollak lost interest in her, she may have regretted this
act of love. Her father disapproved of her passion for
a German Jew and forced his daughter to go into the
sanatorium of Veleslavin to protect her from him. In
vain. Milena was determined to lead her life the way
she wanted.

At eleven, soon after the death of her mother she
entered the *lycée* for girls in Prague, the Minerva
School. Many years later, a former student who had
become a journalist remembered her arrival: 'How
stylish both of them were! The father was carrying
her schoolbag and walked her to the gate . . . I can still
see her, as if it were today, with her grey suit and her
wide-brimmed, dark velvet hat, raised in front and
pulled down in back, with a ribbon on it that floated
in the wind. It went so well with her curly blonde hair
and emphasized the gentleness of her profile and her
transparent skin . . .'

I told Clémence that elegance would define
that woman all through her life. It wasn't only sarto-
rial elegance, even if the young Milena did give it a

certain importance, but the elegance of her whole person and of her engagements, up to her last days in Ravensbrück. I added that I had done several portraits of her for different magazines, each time with the feeling that one could multiply them without ever getting to know her completely. It was in her articles that she seemed to reveal her true personality, her love of life, her perception of men and women embarked in the flight of days, in the war, in sorrows great and small. We laughed a lot, Clémence and I, when Milena related, humorously, her adventures with Madame Kohler, her concierge. 'A year ago, inspired by who knows what noble ideas of equality and fraternity, I suggested that she stop robbing me . . .' But she added, 'She never takes more than she needs, and her needs are modest . . .' We shared her view of happiness, of everything that energized her; we talked about all this for a long time. Clémence was passionately interested in the tragic period of the last war; her whole life was marked by it.

She loved those *written kisses*, the name Kafka gave the letters he sent to Milena, general delivery, letters Milena would pick up under the name of Madame Kramer. We had spent long hours reading them, reading her columns, and all that time brought us closer together; I clearly remember the day I chose these few lines: 'As a little girl, I lived madly waiting for life to begin. I thought that one day, suddenly, life would begin and open up before me like the curtain rising in the theatre, like a show about to start. Nothing happened and many things happened but never what I had hoped for, you couldn't say it was life; and I guess I've persisted in being a little girl, for I keep waiting for that life to come.'

Clémence had interrupted me almost feverishly. 'There was a dune,' she said, 'very long and high, and wooden houses perched on top of it, very small houses, hardly bigger than beach cabins. I was thirteen, we were on vacation, my parents and I. My father had built one of those houses for us. In the one next door there was Paul and his parents, but we didn't know each other. In the mornings, we would be alone, looking at the sea, not entirely awake, waiting for our parents to get up and not daring to come closer to each other. The beach was deserted; I can still remember that strong smell that would sometimes make me queasy, the smell of the tide. One day, Paul came over and asked me if I would go swimming with him. I didn't know how to swim, so he wanted to teach me. Every morning we would run into the waves together; he held me in his arms to reassure me. Then, little by little, we began taking long walks along the beach, he read *Vaillant* to me, *The Blue Men*, he told me that he accompanied his father to all the political demonstrations and when he was older he would join the Party himself. I thought he was handsome, and he was. I liked it when he held me close. At the end of the vacation, they left before us. I cried for hours, I wanted Paul; my mother told me we'd see each other again the following year and we had our whole life before us. Yes, I remember that phrase well, "You have your whole life before you." What was a whole life? Like your Milena, I, too, wondered if it had begun, and if it had, Paul and I didn't have it all to ourselves, so I suspected my mother was lying . . .'

'The following year, they returned and we never left each other. We would sometimes walk for whole days along those endless beaches and I thought my life was beginning right there, I could feel it growing in my changing body: breasts, hips, I didn't dare look at myself in the mirror any more, I had the impression that it wasn't me. I wondered if Paul noticed how much I was being transformed. In the autumn, his parents came to live in Paris, where his father had been appointed. The next three years went by as in a dream that ended the day he died. As on the beach, we would take long walks through the city, and that's probably why I did so much walking later on. We wouldn't talk much at those times, we just held hands and I tried to remember everything, everything seemed so overwhelmingly important then . . .'

'Maybe it's because he's dead that I keep waiting for life to begin, I think I've always been waiting for that life, I mean, life with him. The other life, the one I lived, was something else, it was while I waited . . . Now I'm a very old little girl . . . But you, it seems to me you grew up too, am I wrong?'

I confessed that for a long time I thought I had grown up, but I wasn't so sure any more. She wanted to know more, she wanted to know what kind of little girl I had been. I felt immensely embarrassed and didn't know what to answer, as if my childhood had disappeared, as if it had never existed or had dissolved, quietly, in the years that followed. Then I said:

'A path—that whole time was left on a little country path, a stony dirt path lined with hedges and trees whose shadows fascinated me. Yes, what I think of is the shadows of the trees on that path, they made such an impression on me that I avoided stepping on them, I would walk around them, convinced they were the spirit of the trees and their language, too. On days when the sky was cloudy, their absence worried me. My grandmother Jeanne claimed she knew that language and invented stories in which the trees held back their shadows because they were sad or angry. We would go talk to them, she and I, we would ask them to forgive us if we had done something wrong. Jeanne was a lovely woman; she looked at the world in a state of constant, dazzled wonderment, and she had the gift of transmitting it to me. She loved the earth, the rain, the wind. I think I was a little girl only with her, and on that path; I have no other memories; at least no other memory seems to speak of me at that age . . .'

'Sometimes, at night, we would go out with her dog, Z, to the banks of the river. She wanted to teach me how to tame the night. Sitting at the edge of the water, we would listen to the rustling of nature and it would follow me back home and all the way into my dreams . . . Later, in a museum, I discovered Cézanne's painting, *The House of Doctor Gachet in Auvers*, and I burst into tears—the path and the house slightly hidden by the trees was exactly the image that used to greet me when I came back from our walks. Jeanne had just died; I was still an adolescent and would never return to that house again.'

We remained in Milena's company for several days. Clémence wanted us to 're-invite' her on a regular basis. Her death in a concentration camp upset her tremendously, and so did the pain of her last years, when illness never left her. But, like me, what touched her the most was her love for life, her whimsical spirit, which lent all the more importance to her commitments. We loved her like a true friend. When I returned, if it was a good day and her memory wasn't asleep, Clémence would ask for her before I could even tell her about my trip. And as we did every time, we would begin by the crossing of the Moldau.

*

A strange night was waiting for me at the hotel, too agitated, too short as well: I had to leave before dawn. I paced around my room, packing and unpacking my bag, unable to lie down and wait for sleep—and besides, I didn't feel like sleeping at all. I went down to the bar; I preferred hearing people talk around me, hearing the music of the words a little longer. I would miss the language, as I had missed others upon some of my returns, a strange, painful absence, a kind of break-up. For a few days, everything gets mixed up, thought is blurred and wanders between two languages, the world is torn apart and then, little by little, the voyage finds its place in memory, in everyday life, and everything fades away. What remains is what counted—the places where memories come and go and pull us off into nomadic daydreams.

I was the only customer at the bar. The radio was playing an old Joe Dassin tune sung in Russian! I was trying to put together a few ideas for a letter to Gyl. I was telling him about his child, asking if some day he would read him *The Seven Muzhiks*, the Russian equivalent of the *Tour de France by Two Children*, a book we had bought at the flea market in Vanves a long time ago and I had noticed on his bookshelf. But no, I would speak neither of *The Seven Muzhiks* or of

the *Tour de France by Two Children*; that could be interpreted as an expression of angry disappointment.
What I was feeling was not disappointment, but
rather a feeling of being far away, of a second separation, this one more radical than the first because
of that child. I imagined that he would make kites
for him and, later, take him out on Lake Baikal to
fish for omul; they would be happy, and I sincerely
wanted that. I hoped Irina and he would choose a
Russian name for him and not one of those we had
thought of in case we made the decision to become
parents one day (we knew perfectly well that we
never would). I would not speak of my worries con-
cerning him, of his prolonged silence; I would tell
him about the days and nights on the train, about
Igor and Boris, I would tell him about the Globus and
the night outing on the Angara, I would say nothing
about Volya. I would probably never send this letter,
or any other.

When I got back to the room, there were barely
two hours left. Leaning on the windowsill, I watched
the dark flow of the Angara. The sleeping street made
me anxious; I could hear from afar a vague humming
and I wondered if the woman was singing 'Suliko', if
it was her voice that was spreading through the city.
Steps were coming nearer and someone knocked on
the door. The boy from the bar held out a piece of
paper and said, 'Boris.' 'He's still here?' I asked. *Niet.*

I ran to the window. No one. The boy had already disappeared and the paper was on the bed. *The Hills of Manchuria*, all the lyrics, signed Boris. I went down into the street to try and catch him: I felt elated by his gesture and I wanted to tell him, kiss him, hug him as we did when we left each other. No Boris in sight. I looked all over the neighbourhood without realizing that I had let myself go all the way to Volya's. The woman wasn't singing, her window was closed and her house silent, but Volya's house seemed quite animated: a large group of people was laughing and talking loudly. Why not say goodbye to her before I took the plane and thank her again for welcoming me?

It wasn't Volya who opened the door but a huge, corpulent man. Volya was sitting at a table along with a dozen or so people. She noticed me and waved me over, introducing me as a friend of Gyl. Immediately, all faces turned to me, everyone heaped compliments on him. I smiled at everyone, wondering what role I was playing in whatever life Gyl had made for himself since he arrived here. I had the same feeling as in his house—I felt I didn't belong and had no right to claim any connection to him.

Volya asked if I had found him in the village and I answered that he was travelling with his wife. She did not seem to know of Irina's existence, her face froze, she said something to her neighbour and I realized that the news was upsetting her greatly. 'He won't come back,' she said, 'now I know he won't come back.' How strange that voyage was! I had not been able to find Gyl but had learnt about the private life he never mentioned in his letters. I don't know what compelled me to add that they were expecting a child, but when I saw Volya's eyes fill with tears, I felt that she was relieving me of my own pain. I wasn't very proud of myself, all the more so as the day I'd arrived in Irkutsk, I was perfectly aware of the effect Gyl had on her. Her emotion when I said his name spoke volumes. Her neighbour put her arm around her and shot me a hostile look. 'Do you know the name of his wife?' Volya asked. I answered that her name was Irina. She said something to the woman next to her again and I realized Irina had been her children's teacher, and sometimes Gyl drove them to school. I no longer felt comfortable among these people—Volya's distress had silenced them. I came over to her to say goodbye and apologize for what I had just told her, I had no way of knowing . . . She got up and kissed me, sobbing, I hugged her hard and said, 'That's the way he is.'

Why did I say those words? How could I speak of him like that after more than twenty years of separation? I had just destroyed everything that had been the way we were together, outside codes, outside everything that gave society the right to exploit love and make it one of the cogs in its machine. Irina and the child changed nothing in what we had been, did not negate it; I alone was actually erasing it. I wanted to make up for those clumsy words but found nothing, I just whispered into Volya's ear that he had loved her and he'd even written that to me. Her sobs redoubled; it was high time for me to get out of this dead end. I could read a growing hostility in people's looks and I suddenly noticed one of Volya's children in a doorway, in pyjamas, with a sleepy face, watching his mother cry. I hated myself. The same man who had opened the door for me walked me to the street and asked me to say nothing to Gyl. What image did he have of me, did he think I'd come with the intention of hurting Volya, or that Gyl had sent me in his place to put an end to an affair that was getting in his way? I didn't answer. I remembered the morning Lise had called me to say that Gyl was sleeping at her place, she was determined to keep him and if I tried anything to put an end to their relationship I would regret it. I had smiled: Gyl had warned me, he had told me about her and I did not feel betrayed. I said so to Lise, whose voice had suddenly failed her, perhaps she was crying. I hung up.

As I walked back to the hotel, it was as if I was back in that time when Gyl and I were always going through violent crises, where each one wanted complete freedom and couldn't stand the other person's

freedom. At the time, Gyl had a number of simulta-
neous affairs and went mad when I did the same
thing. We were stubbornly seeking an impossible
balance and were actually on the road to ruin. But I
had loved and still loved the certainty that there are
no great ideas without love, without freedom, and
our desperate attempts to prove it had not been in
vain. In fact, it was the only thing that gave our relationship meaning. I had actually never given that up,
and what was tormenting me was the impression
that I could no longer be on that perpetual quest. Perhaps that's what growing old meant—no longer
seeking an impossible balance.

Could *Irina* be that possible balance?

The taxi was waiting in front of the hotel.

*

My last visit to Clémence on the eve of my departure did not go as it usually did. She wasn't sitting on her sofa; it was as if she'd been watching for me from behind her door. Hardly had I rung the bell than she was opening the door and asking why I wasn't coming to see her any more. The young woman who kept her company during the day was standing a few steps away from her and I could see worry and fatigue in her eyes. I tried to explain that I had come three days earlier, but she no longer remembered. 'Milena was with us,' I added, 'we read one of her adventures with Madame Kohler, remember Madame Kohler and her fiancé, Joseph the shoemaker? Don't you remember?'

'*Madame Kohler, where is my husband's shirt?*'

'*Joseph put it on today.*'

'*But Madame Kohler . . .*'

'*Well, I had no way of knowing that Monsieur would want to wear it today.*'

She had me there. She really had no way of knowing.

Clémence remembered nothing and that was happening more and more often. Her memory fluctuated from one day to the next: it would waver and then return, to disappear again.

'And the way she swam across the Moldau, Clémence, the story you like so much, that date with her lover when she absolutely wanted to be on time, remember?' 'No, that's me,' she said, with the same aplomb as the time we spoke of it before, 'I'm the one who swam towards him, to meet him . . .'

Without protesting, I abandoned Milena for Marion du Faouët, reconstituted her life story very slowly, step by step, from her birth in Porz en Haie, doing the markets with her mother, the Jaffré sisters who had tried in vain to give her a bourgeois education, up to the army of men on horseback that she had formed and her ritual refrain, 'Your money or your life, please', for, contrary to a certain Marie Collin alias Marie l'Escalier, she never shed blood and in fact, most of the time, no complaint was ever lodged against her. I described the rides on horseback through the Arrée mountains, her fatal fall at Hennebont with Henri Pezron, her trial in 1747, how he was put to the question and hanged on Place des Lices, while she was beaten, branded and led naked through the city. An ordeal which did not deter her from taking up arms again . . . Do you remember that you often called her 'that gutsy girl'? My story disturbed her: it awakened something in her but failed to lift that fog in which she was getting lost.

I pulled her over to the sofa and sat down on my chair. I slipped a hand into the secret of the red velvet, took out the photo of the Quai de Bourbon and showed it to her. 'Paul and Clémence, 1943, you remember Paul?' Her pained look froze with the fruitless effort. Then I described the little houses on the dunes, the mornings when she and Paul would wait for their parents to wake up while they watched the movements of the sea, the flight of the gulls in the big northern sky. I reminded her of the day when Paul asked her to go swimming with him for the first time, how he held her in his arms and how much she loved to feel his body against hers. She finally smiled and whispered, 'How do you know all that, how did you guess?' I was as moved as the day she had said to me, 'You're lucky to have someone to think about,' but above all I realized that despite her doctor's attention, her condition was deteriorating.

Could I remind her that I was leaving the next morning, while she huddled up on her sofa as if every word I spoke was throwing her into a state of terrible helplessness and confusion, and she was trying to protect herself from it?

But a kind of miracle happened. I got up and walked towards her old workshop, asking her to tell me about her trade with a few more details than the first time, the time we had tried on a few hats, but she couldn't remember it at all. Her face lit up, she jumped up to open the door on the magnificent disorder inside and suddenly the gestures and words came back to her and she explained how, from the initial bell-shaped felt delivered to her, she would make the silhouette of a hat by working with a steam iron, how she would then choose the decorative elements, the little details that made it distinctive—a feather, a veil, a flower—always considering what the latest fashion was at the time, and sometimes copying models she had seen in shop windows she had passed on her walks. On her insistence, I tried on all the hats in the closet again, and again she wanted me to choose one; no point telling her she had already given me a panama hat, she didn't want to hear about it. I gave in and took the wide-brimmed hat made of rice straw that made me look like a lady in a summer resort.

After that guided tour, she was exhausted but thrilled. Before we went out of her workshop, she asked me when I was leaving to go find my friend. 'Over there, very far away,' she added. Her question left me dumbfounded. I looked at her with such astonishment that she said with a detached air, 'Aren't you leaving on a long trip?'

As I thought back over those moments on the way to the airport, I wondered if she was going to recognize me. It was the first time that thought had come to mind; it took hold of me all at once and everything suddenly seemed extremely fragile. I was watching the sun rising in the morning mist; the world could disappear from one moment to the next.

*

The stopover in Moscow turned into several hours of waiting due to technical problems. Little by little, I sank into a state of somnolence conducive to daydreaming. Everything was blurred together, exacerbating my impatience—an impatience with no particular object except the desire to be elsewhere, to leave this country the way you leave a lover who has betrayed you. I saw myself again with Gyl after he had announced his intention of leaving, reading that phrase of Pessoa's to him: 'I would be capable of going to live in Siberia for the sole pleasure of becoming averse to the idea . . .' I laughed to provoke him but he disliked the way I was reacting to his announcement, for I was one of the rare people to whom he was confiding his plan. I swore I wouldn't take for my own what the author of *The Keeper of Flocks* had written, but I added that I didn't like what I saw as an escape, and reading that sentence was my way of telling him that, with humour and without getting into useless discussions. We did have those discussions anyway. They reminded me of others, old ones, which had got the better of us. I should have known that there was already a distance between us, even before the kilometres added to it, but I wanted to maintain a connection to this man who counted in my life. I listened to his arguments: I would have liked to be convinced but I was moved by his determination not to abandon everything that had given meaning to our struggles, even in that country which had ruined all our hopes.

In his first letters, he challenged my reservations. He wanted to show me it was still possible to go forward despite all the obstacles. I didn't respond to these allegations, I simply assured him of my affectionate support and was sure he didn't doubt it. I informed him of what was happening in that country where a former KGB man had all the power. He replied that he knew it—he wasn't naive—but that didn't affect what he was planning to do.

I knew how stubborn he was. I remembered several occasions when his stubbornness had opposed us. I also remembered another wait in an airport— the plane from Chile Gyl was on hadn't arrived. I was desperately trying to get some explanation. Other friends were waiting with me but we couldn't share our anxieties, so we didn't speak. And then the plane landed. I looked for his face in the crowd coming out of the plane, I saw it, he was smiling at me from afar, I was madly in love, we had been living together for a short time and life would never end. He emerged from the crowd and I ran into his arms. We left the others to their effusions, didn't exchange a word until we got to our studio apartment on Rue Ordener, went up the endless flight of stairs, opened the door and dived into the heart of our kingdom. A kingdom cluttered with books, posters, the leaflets we were going to hand out to workers as they came out of their factories outside Paris, jazz records and objects collected here and there in the course of our walks.

The bed made its way through this rough sea, it was our universe, the only possible place for everything. For years, we had lived on this tiny planet and when the time came to leave it because we no longer knew how to live in it together, both of us felt like we were being exiled. Later, when we reminisced about those years, we would always say, 'Up there, remember, we were still up there?'

I had fallen asleep on the plane. I was in the midst of the children of Lake Baikal, our heads raised to watch the flight of the kites gliding above us. Gyl was there, too, he was giving orders and advice, carrying a child on his shoulders—his child—and I was asking him what his name was; his name was Igor. He held him out to me, I took him in my arms, he smelt of milk and raspberry. I spoke to him in Russian, he was heavy, very heavy and I gave him back to Gyl who was walking away and disappearing behind the dachas. I went into one of them and at the end of a long corridor, there was Clémence sitting on her red sofa. She was singing 'Suliko' with the same voice as the woman in Irkutsk and didn't seem to recognize me. I walked over to her anyway and told her my name was Anne, but she kept on singing without paying any attention to me, and then suddenly disappeared. I sat down at her place on the sofa, put my hand between the back and the seat and touched the photo without daring to take it out of its hiding place.

The wind was growing so strong that it was making the open window bang behind the sofa. I looked at the waves it was raising on the lake, I heard the children shouting because the kites were getting away from them and crashing on the surface of the water. They ran to get them, I saw them charging forward and swimming up to those many-coloured wrecks, trying to bring them back to the shore. I went out and called for them to come have their afternoon snack. They were pushing each other as they came into the house, a joyful, noisy scramble that woke me up. The plane had just landed.

*

The driver of the taxi was talking on the phone in a language I couldn't identify, although it did seem to me that it could be one of the languages of the Baltic countries. From his tone, I guessed there was a woman at the other end of the line and they were exchanging words of love. I would have liked him to drive faster but didn't dare interrupt that babble. When we arrived in front of my building, he turned around to apologize, 'She's bored,' he said with a broad smile, and I smiled in return. I got out, went into the lobby and rushed up the stairs to the third floor. The door was open and from each side there rose columns of cardboard boxes. I walked over, stepped into the hallway with some apprehension, but was far from imagining the surprise that awaited me. At the very end of the corridor, sitting on the sofa with her legs dangling, a little girl was reading a magazine aloud. She was wearing a hat whose veil hid her face. The old little girl—that was my first thought, a mad thought that I corrected immediately. The hats were scattered around the girl; some were on the floor, others emerged from open cartons.

With my back against the wall, I watched the child stumble through a cooking recipe, corrected from time to time by a feminine voice coming from

the workshop, 'Mix . . . the . . . in-gre-di-ents un-til
. . . What's ingredients?' asked the little girl, without
lifting her nose from the magazine. A young woman
appeared at the door of the workshop, ready to
answer. She was carrying a pile of felt hats of all
colours that she set down on one of the boxes and our
eyes met. The little girl picked up the veil of the hat
and was looking at me, too. I couldn't speak, couldn't
believe what I was seeing; I might have thought I was
on the wrong floor if the red sofa hadn't convinced
me of the contrary.

Today it seems to me that for a long time nothing happened. The wall was holding me up and the
little girl and the woman seemed to be very far away
at the end of the hall, everything was blurring, what
with the fatigue of the trip and the night of insomnia
that had preceded it. Then the woman walked over
to me. 'Yes?' was all she said, in a rather curt tone.

'Clémence, I was coming to see Clémence.'

'She's not here any more,' she answered while
the little girl was resuming her halting reading of
the magazine, 'Spread . . . out . . . the . . . dough . . .
with . . .'

I was still motionless, I didn't dare to ask for
more details, I couldn't imagine that Clémence had
moved during my absence. On the other hand, the
doctor might have thought it a good idea, given her
condition, to put her into an institution. But the

young woman interrupted my thoughts: 'Who are you?'

The little girl then stopped reading and said in a high-pitched voice with that fake childish innocence which sometimes chills you to the bone, 'She's dead, Mommy, right Mommy, isn't she dead?'

'She passed away, a week ago now,' the young woman confirmed.

'What's passed away, is it because she's dead?'

'That means the same thing, yes,' her mother answered.

I slipped my hand into the velvet folds. The photo was there. This contact annulled everything, it negated death, and something impossible to explain was making Clémence present. She was there. I came to and explained who I was, a neighbour who came to read to her from time to time. We were rather close and I was returning from a trip; I had promised to come see her as soon as I got back.

The young lady then took me out on the landing to tell me what had happened. A few days after I left, at daybreak Clémence had asked the night nurse to take her out on the same walk she and I had taken together before to the Quai de Bourbon. The night nurse didn't dare refuse, she called a taxi and accompanied her to the quay. But once they were there, Clémence had sent her to tell the driver not to wait for them, they would call another taxi later. It was during her brief absence that Clémence had fallen into the water.

I remember listening to the story the young woman was telling me with a kind of bewilderment, for it spoke to me of something else, something I was the only one to know, something intimate that bound us together, Clémence and I. That fall into the Seine was not an accident, it was a date, a date that, in a certain sense, she was making with me, too, and because of that I felt less pain. I was sure Clémence wanted me to understand what she had done. She was counting on me to understand, I was sure of it.

The young woman seemed surprised at how distraught I was, and she probably found my reaction excessive. After all, for me, Clémence was only an old neighbour, someone I used to spend a bit of time with. She herself had never known her. The family, at least what was left of it, had practically no ties with one another, and in fact none at all with Clémence.

The little girl stopped reading aloud and her mother asked me to follow her back into the apartment; she wanted to make sure the child wasn't doing anything silly. She was sleeping, stretched out on the sofa, with the hat covering her face.

'All this is exhausting for her, she doesn't understand why we're here, in a place she doesn't know,' the young woman whispered, putting her finger on her lips to invite me to talk softly, too. I had nothing to say, I was just remembering that afternoon when Clémence could no longer climb the stairs; we had laughed madly like two kids, shaking with laughter, stuck between two floors. We were coming back from the cafe across the street and hadn't drink to excess, but a glass of white wine at that time of day had a rather euphoric effect on us. We nonetheless managed to reach the third floor and I walked her over to the sofa. First she asked for another anecdote about Madame Kohler, then fell asleep. I helped her stretch out on the seat, which put her in the same position as the little girl.

I didn't dare tell her mother how much her daughter resembled Clémence. Her pointy face, her clear complexion, that mischievous way she had of looking at things and people brought her back to me with such intensity it was rather disturbing. Her lips and eyelids had little quivers that suggested she was pretending to be asleep. And in fact she jumped up, put away the hat and veil and stared at me while she grabbed her mother's hand.

'What's your name?' I asked her.

'Marion.'

She simpered so naturally that it made her irresistibly amusing.

A gutsy girl, I thought.

*

I didn't go to the Quai de Bourbon the first day, or the second. I was preparing myself for it, as if for another trip. It never stopped raining; the summer was slowly dying and giving the city that sweet languor that is so becoming to it, sometimes. The young woman came to say goodbye; the apartment would be emptied by a junk dealer because nothing really interested her except for the hats and felt. She had forgotten to introduce herself the day before—she was the granddaughter of one of Clémence's cousins, and I didn't dare ask anything else about that vague family Clémence never talked about.

'What about the sofa, is it also going to the dealer?' I asked.

'Yes, are you interested in it?'

'Something does interest me—a photo. Clémence kept it between the seat and the back of the sofa. It was a secret between us and I'd love to have it.'

She led me into the apartment and I showed her the photo. Afterwards, I never took it out of its new hiding place at the back of one of my drawers. I thought that in the absence of Clémence it was unavailable to me. I just liked knowing it was there.

It was only on the third day that I dared approach the quay. I finally went there, but first lingered on the Louis-Philippe Bridge. It was very early, like on the morning Clémence and I had leant over the water and she showed me the spot where she and Paul had come to rest one Sunday after a long walk through the city. She remembered that he was anxious that day, he spoke even less than usual and she didn't dare ask anything. She knew you couldn't ask questions. On the way, they had run into a friend of Paul's who accompanied them to the quay; he was the one who took the photo. He was also the one who was assassinated on the street with Paul.

I was alone on the bridge. The sky and roofs were fusing into a gentle, pearly grey. After two days of rain, the Seine was carrying a muddy water that came biting into the edges of the banks. I didn't dare go down to the river, I only walked along the parapet, staring down at the tumultuous current rushing by under the bridge. I was looking for the spot where Clémence had chosen to throw herself off to go meet Paul; it was probably the spot where they had been sitting that Sunday—their last one. She had gone down the stairs with the young night nurse behind her, it was cool out, and they could hear the humming of the taxi's engine above their heads. And then Clémence had turned towards the young woman and asked her to tell the driver there was no point waiting for them, they'd find another taxi.

I could see Clémence's frail silhouette standing out on the riverbank and the young woman disappearing behind the parapet to dismiss the driver. I could hear the birds chirping just as we had heard them on that other morning, I remembered we had looked at the same trees, the same magnificent buildings along this quay, the same image of the Ile Saint-Louis whose prow advanced on the river like a ship arriving safe and sound.

I imagined someone going over to a window (the man the little girl's mother had told me about) and discovering the scene—two women, one quite old and the other less so, hanging around near the water, on that Quai de Bourbon, so peaceful at that hour. The taxi must have disturbed his sleep and he was trying to understand the reason for these unusual presences at such an early time. And then, perhaps, he had suddenly seen Clémence let herself sink into the abyss and disappear into the swift current of the river that had just emerged from the night. He thought at first he hadn't seen right, the woman hadn't dived, she wasn't there and he'd imagined her act in a drowsy state which he was now trying to shake off. But the younger woman who was crying for help, running along the bank of the river with her arms raised to heaven, threw herself on the ground in despair and remained prostrate for a few seconds before going up the stairs shouting again: 'Help!' He had opened the window and everything had started: the firemen, the paramedics, the police, a whole noisy ballet that turned the quay upside down.

Clémence had taken as her own Milena's swim across the Moldau several times before—that wild drive towards the man she loved thrilled her. I could easily imagine her having that impulse, I was even sure of it. She had dived into the water to make up for all that time without Paul. She would meet him again. She'd been waiting for that meeting for such a long time.

I stood there scrutinizing the riverbank until the first sightseeing boats appeared, until the long line of cars started along the river and the first pedestrians crossed the bridge in both directions—until all the noise and bustle shook the city out of its torpor. I put off going down the stairs to the quay until the next day. I needed time for my date with Clémence. I knew it would not be a date with sadness and sorrow, but a date with life.

*

The next day, sitting on the first steps of the stairway leading down to the riverbank, I was watching the shimmering surface of the water. The leaves of the trees, still green, held the golden light of the end of summer that glinted in the reflections constantly shifting with the moving current. I was caught between the insistent memory of my journey and the desire to be with Clémence. Little by little the two had come together, and at this moment defined my life. I did not leave my observation post for a long time. I saw, in the water flowing before my eyes, chaotic images of these last months, from the time I met Clémence until this journey from which I had not completely returned.

Before reaching the stairs, I passed the plaque saying that Camille Claudel had lived and worked in that building on the Quai de Bourbon. I reread the sentence she had written to Rodin: 'There is always something missing that torments me.'

Too much sorrow, too much solitude in the life of Camille Claudel, despite her mad passion for Rodin and the exhilarating, effervescent times when only sculpture mattered. One day, life had shattered; it now stretched out endlessly before her in the convent at Montdevergues, where Camille never stopped waiting for another Paul, the brother who rarely came to see her: always elsewhere, at the four corners of the globe, even to the banks of Lake Baikal, taking the same train that was still rocking me. Unhappiness and resignation, that's how her life had ended—a sister left to her despair by that adored brother, by her mother too, indifferent to the suffering of her daughter. She would die in her forced reclusion. Camille and Clémence, two women with nothing in common. Despite her age and forced immobility, the idea of happiness was still alive in Clémence. She was still in love with life, always ready to seize a luminous moment, to make the effort to walk down two flights of stairs to raise a glass of white wine in honour of our beloved women. Camille would have driven her to despair—her emotional exile, her submission to misery, and then, Paul—that name—that absence which was, for her, the echo of another. I wanted to protect her from it. Camille's ghost may have been wandering around this place, but Clémence had come here because it was a beautiful, happy Sunday.

Siberia, the train, Igor and Boris, Lake Baikal and Irkutsk insisted on pulling me far from this quay, and I did not push them away; they mingled harmoniously with the melancholy of those moments.

'I find you quite melancholy today,' Clémence had said to me on one of those days when I was beginning to get worried about Gyl. I replied that she was right, but melancholy was a rather pleasant state to be in. The next day, I brought her these lines by Madame Roland from 1771: 'The sweet melancholy I am defending is never sad, it is merely a modification of pleasure, whose charms it borrows . . . Melancholy imparts something noble, a striking colouration, to a wild perspective, to a lonely forest.' Clémence had asked me if Madame Roland knew Olympe de Gouges; I had no idea, but it was not impossible.

Alone on those steps, I was precisely in the sweet melancholy of that time so special to me, the passage from one age to another that Clémence had helped me cross, without knowing it. I was sure that what she had done was not a desperate act; it was, on the contrary, a living, intensely beautiful act—her last. She had found the energy she'd lacked for some time and appropriated Milena's amorous dive completely. What Milena had done was, for her, the consummate expression of immoderate love. We had never really exchanged views about death—the deaths of our heroines probably enabled us to avoid pointless talk about our own. We were simply content to share our immense admiration for the excesses of those passionate women who had faced death unflinchingly.

I don't know how long I remained like that, wandering from one thought to another. I had never felt as close to Clémence, as attached to her, to what she had given me ever since the day I had rung her doorbell for the first time.

A man's voice suddenly brought me out of my reverie.

'You're the one who was with the old lady who drowned last week, right?'

He had his elbows on the parapet and was leaning out above me.

'I've been watching you for some time,' he went on, 'and I told myself that maybe you feel guilty, but I saw everything, you couldn't guess what was going to happen, I witnessed it myself and I couldn't believe it. I'll tell you, she went into the water like in a dream, she let herself slip into it, she didn't disappear right away, no more than a few seconds, you'd think someone was holding her above the water. That's why I waited for you to show up, it was, how can I say it, unreal, calm, yes, calm. She didn't throw herself into the water, you might say the water took her and kept her. Are you in the family?'

I answered yes, he was right. Now I, too, thought it was a peaceful, quiet act. She just needed to be accompanied. I didn't correct his mistake—the night nurse was blonde like me, and slender, too; he wasn't totally awake that morning.

I left, but I knew that the next morning I would go down to the riverbank and it would be our last meeting. Then I decided it would also be our last reading. I liked the idea of coming to read to Clémence one more time, at the spot where we would part for ever. As on the first day, I spent the night looking for a text she would like, and as I was looking I thought of what Robert Walser had written to a friend: 'I love life, but I love it because I hope it will give me the chance to throw it overboard with dignity.'

*

*

I went back to the quay with three stanzas by Nazim Hikmet. She would like those verses, imbued with a sense of everyday life, the life that drives you, from one day to the next, to uncertain shores.

I walked down to the riverbank, sat down by the water, and read, as if she could hear me, as if she were sitting by my side:

> We stand over the water,
> the plane tree, me, the cat, the sun and our lives.
> Our image appears in the water:
> the plane tree, me, the cat, the sun and our lives.
>
> We stand over the water,
> the cat will go first,
> in the water his image will be lost.
> And then I myself will go away,
> in the water my image will be lost.
> And then the plane tree will go,
> in the water its image will be lost.
> And then the water will go away,
> the sun will remain,
> And then it, too, will go.
>
> We stand over the water,
> the plane tree, me, the cat, the sun and our lives.

The water is cool,
the plane tree is huge,
I write these verses
the cat dozes,
thank God we are alive,
the reflection of the water touches us,
the plane tree, me, the cat, the sun and our lives.

I got up, and I saw the man watching me and smiling, sitting on the first step of the stairs. 'There are stanzas missing,' he said. 'The first three.'

He had dark blue eyes that I hadn't noticed the day before.

*

When we sleep at his place, in the room overlooking the quay, at daybreak I sometimes go to the window and stare into the Seine. The memory of Clémence never ceases to accompany me. It shines on the surface of the water.

Then I slip back inside the big bed where the man is still sleeping. He holds out a hand and puts it on me. I think of the earth after the rain, of ports, of trains, of rivers, of children at a lakeside, of early mornings on a beach under the shade of the trees . . .

Translators' Notes

p. 23

Quelque part dans l'inachevé (Somewhere in the Unfinished), a work by the philosopher Vladimir Jankélévitch published in 1978 by Gallimard.

p. 50

A la lisière du temps (At the Edge of Time), a volume of poems by Claude Roy, was published in 1984 by Gallimard.

p. 51

'Chien et Loup' ('Dog and Wolf') is a poem found in *A la lisière du temps*. The colloquial expression 'between dog and wolf' means 'At twilight'.

p. 73

The Blue Men was a comic strip in the communist youth magazine *Vaillant*.

To Paule